She didn't know she w
destroy both their worl

"I'm not going to leave my home!"

Torian jerked Sara toward him. The porch light shone down on her. He could see the faint gold flecks in her gaze, could see smooth beauty of her skin. And the fierce determination on her face.

"Sara..." He knew it would be hard for her. She would be leaving the life, the friends, she'd known. The world he'd show her would be far different from this one.

"No." She shook her head quickly. "I'm not going. Find somebody else."

Damn. This was going to be harder than he'd thought. But there really was no choice. He had to protect her. "I'm sorry," he whispered. "I hope you can understand."

Her eyes widened. "Understand what?"

He didn't answer. He reached up and stroked her cheek. Her skin was so warm. So soft. His gaze fell to his lips. Such perfect red, full lips. And he remembered how she'd tasted.

His head lowered toward her. He needed to kiss her again, just one more time. Torian expected her to pull away. To fight him.

Instead she met him, her lips parting instantly for the thrust of his tongue. His arms wrapped around her as he pulled her close. His mouth fed on hers. God, she tasted like sweet wine.

His tongue slid deep into the warmth of her mouth. He couldn't get enough of her. Had to have more.

Torian fought for his control. Now wasn't the time. He couldn't have her. Not yet.

Slowly, so slowly, he lifted his head, breathing heavily. She stared up at him, her mouth swollen from his kisses.

Sara wet her lips. "That...doesn't change...anything." Her chin lifted. "I'm not...going anywhere...with you."

Her pulse pounded furiously at the base of her throat. Torian could see the faint tremors that shook her body. He stroked her shoulders. "Sara...I don't remember giving you a choice."

For Nicholas, the man who gave me a
happy ending of my own. I love you.

Other books by Cynthia Eden

The Vampire's Kiss

The Wizard's Spell

***

Cynthia Eden

The Wizard's Spell
Published by ImaJinn Books

ISBN: 1-933417-13-7

10 9 8 7 6 5 4 3 2 1

PUBLISHER'S NOTE:
This book is a work of fiction. Names, characters, places and incidents are products of the author's imagination or are used fictitiously. Any resemblance to actual events or locales or persons, living or dead, is entirely coincidental.

Books are available at quantity discounts when used to promote products or services. For information please write to: Marketing Division, ImaJinn Books, P.O. Box 545, Canon City, CO 81212, or call toll free 1-877-625-3592.

Cover design by Rickey Mallory

ImaJinn Books
P.O. Box 545, Canon City, CO 81212
Toll Free: 1-877-625-3592
http://www.imajinnbooks.com

Prologue

"You realize, of course, that the Dark Ones will be looking for her, too."

The wizard nodded.

The small, white-haired woman grunted. "You'll have to bring her back."

His stare was cold. Hard. "She may not want to come."

The woman leaned over a fat black cauldron. "That doesn't really matter, does it?"

He shook his head.

Fog drifted lazily from the cauldron. "When do you leave?"

"Tonight." His silver gaze locked on the fog.

"Good." She stared into the cauldron. "Your bride has waited too long as it is."

One

Sara Myers woke with the sudden, shocking certainty that she wasn't alone.

Someone was in her house. In the bedroom. With her.

She could *feel* him, standing there, standing close to her. So close that she could hear the steady sound of his breathing.

Fear pumped through her. Her heart pounded and her hands began to shake.

Oh, my God. Oh, my God. She'd read stories about this. About men breaking into women's homes and attacking them while they slept.

She kept her eyes closed, trying to think, trying to figure out what the hell she should do. She could try screaming. If her neighbor happened to have his hearing aid in, then Carl would have a fifty-fifty shot of hearing her.

Or she could try to fight him. She'd taken a self-defense class at the Y. She knew how to go in hard and fast on a man's weak spots. Oh, yeah, she could fight. Eyes. Ears. Groin—

Then again, maybe he wasn't there to attack her. Maybe he was just a robber. Maybe he just wanted to steal her blind, and if she kept her eyes closed, he'd go away. He'd just go—

The floorboard near her bed squeaked, and Sara shot out from beneath the covers, screaming at the top of her lungs.

A dark shadow lunged for her, and a man's large hand slammed down over her mouth.

The guy was tall and well-muscled. She could feel his body pressing against hers. She threw her hands up, trying to press her thumbs into his eyes.

He growled and twisted away from her. Her nails raked across his face, and she lifted her knee, preparing to deliver as hard a hit to his groin as she could.

"Dammit!" His voice was a grating whisper in the darkness. "Stop it! I'm not here to hurt you!" He took a quick step away from her.

She stumbled back and reached for her nightstand drawer where she kept a Mag flashlight. Carl had given it to her last Christmas. As far as weapons went, it wasn't much. But it was better than nothing.

"You don't need that," he said softly, moving to turn on her overhead light. "I told you, I'm not here to hurt you. There's no need for you to be afraid of me."

She blinked, her eyes adjusting quickly to the sudden flash of light. When she got a good look at the man who had broken into her home, she knew she was in serious trouble. He was, without a doubt, the most dangerous looking man that she'd ever seen.

Physically, his size alone was intimidating. He had to be at least six-foot-two, maybe six-foot-three. His body was thick with muscles, his shoulders broad and strong. His long, pitch black hair was pulled back into some sort of tie at the nape of his neck. He had thin lips and a sharp, almost hawkish, nose. His light silver eyes were glinting and hard, and his jaw was strong, sculpted, and currently clenched.

He wore black leather—a heavy leather coat that clung like a second skin to his wide shoulders. Beneath the open coat, she could see that he wore a simple black shirt and a supple, black pair of pants that melded tightly to his powerful thighs. His feet were encased in high black boots, and a black belt wrapped around his waist. A wickedly sharp knife hung from that belt.

Oh, my God. Her gaze locked on the weapon. The knife was huge. And sharp. And the hilt was covered with jewels.

"Don't be afraid of me, Sara." There was a plea in his voice. "I promise you, I'd never hurt you."

So said the man with the enormous knife. She swallowed and forced her gaze to lift, forced herself to meet that chilling silver stare, and then she realized he'd called her Sara. "H-how do you my name?"

He lifted his hands up, palms forward, and took a hesitant step toward her. "You'd be surprised by the things I know about you."

That wasn't reassuring. She lifted the heavy flashlight, her fingers tightening around its base. She held it like a bat, ready to swing at any moment. "Look, buddy, I-I don't know who you are, but I want you out of my house. *Now!*"

He took another slow, gliding step toward her. "I'm afraid I can't leave."

"Yeah, you can. It's really easy. All you have to do is just walk down the hall and go out the front door. If you go now, I won't even call the cops. We'll just forget this whole thing ever happened." Yeah, right. She'd be on the phone to Sheriff Harty before the nut job in front of her had even left her porch.

His brilliant silver gaze seemed to shimmer. "I can't leave you."

"Sure you can." She sidestepped, trying to head casually

toward the bedroom door. "Just go. You're a big boy, um, I mean guy. You just go right ahead and walk out of my house. I won't stop you." She could feel her knees shaking, but she'd be damned if she'd let this guy see her fear.

"I can't leave you," he repeated softly, his voice a deep rumble. "You're in danger."

Like she hadn't already figured that one out. After all, there was a strange man with a very large knife in her bedroom. If that didn't spell danger, she didn't know what did. Okay. Time to play hardball. She was just steps away from the bedroom door. If she could distract him, she could make a run for it. And she was a good runner. She jogged three times a week around the park.

Her fingers clenched around the base of the flashlight. She wouldn't have much time. She'd have to move fast.

He frowned, studying the raised flashlight with a puzzled expression.

Sara swung the flashlight, hard and fast. She heard him grunt as the weapon made contact with his midsection. He doubled over, and then she ran as fast as she could, heading straight for the door.

She could hear him groaning behind her. A smile stretched across her lips, and she jerked her bedroom door open. Her bare feet slapped against the hardwood floor as she fled down the hall. Just a few more feet. She could see the front door. So close—

He tackled her. Her body was thrown to the floor, and she gasped as all of the air was knocked out of her.

He stretched her arms above her head, and his heavy legs pinned her in place. The leather of his boots rubbed against the skin of her bare legs.

The hardwood pressed against her stomach, and she knew that her shirt had risen beneath her. As usual, she'd been sleeping in an old t-shirt and a pair of shorts. She wished she'd been wearing the ankle length gown her friend Trish had given her for her twenty-ninth birthday. She hated having her body revealed to this stranger.

She bucked beneath him, desperately wanting to be free of him, to escape.

His hands tightened around her wrists. "You shouldn't have done that." The words were spoken into her right ear, and she shivered.

"Let me go," Sara whispered, pulling against his grip. She

couldn't stand being pinned down like this. She jerked, trying to twist her wrists free. "Let me go!" This time, the words were a scream.

He moved in a blur, flipping her over onto her back. She peered up at him, straining to see his features in the shadows.

"Promise me that you won't run again."

"I promise," she said instantly.

She could feel his gaze upon her, feel the weight of that silver stare. She held her breath, hoping that he would believe her, hoping that he would give her freedom. That he would let down his guard for just a moment.

"All right." His body lifted and he reached down, pulling her to her feet. "If you'd just give me a chance to explain—"

She lifted her knee, aiming for the general area of his groin. When she heard him groan in sudden pain, she knew she'd found her mark.

But she didn't waste time congratulating herself. She hopped to her feet, lunged for the door, and fumbled with the lock, turning the deadbolt and then unhooking the chain. She yanked open the door—

And a heavy, hard hand slammed against the wood, effectively shutting the door and trapping her inside.

He grabbed her arm and spun her around. "Dammit, you said you wouldn't run! You promised!" There was anger in his voice. Anger, and a strange hint of hurt. Moonlight trickled through the blinds of a nearby window and illuminated his frowning face.

Her lips curved in a parody of a smile. "I lied." Like she was going to worry about keeping her word to a criminal.

His fingers tightened around her shoulders and a muscle jerked in his jaw. His hair had come loose in their struggle, and dark, heavy black strands clung to the strong planes of his face.

Damn. The man's hair was longer than hers. Her own blond hair was cut in a chin length bob, but his hair fell in thick waves to his shoulders. It was a ridiculous thing to notice, but for some reason, her gaze was drawn to that dark mane of hair. It was so thick, and it looked so smooth.

She took a deep breath. What was wrong with her? A maniac had broken into her house and she was staring at his hair?

Thump.

Thump.

Thump.

Sara felt every muscle in her body tense at that faint sound.

She knew that sound.

Thump.

Thump.

Oh, thank God! It was the sound of Carl's cane on the sidewalk. He must've had his hearing aid in, and the dear, sweet man was coming to her rescue!

Her captor frowned and tilted his head to the side. "What's that sound?"

Sara blinked, hoping her large blue eyes looked innocent. Her grandmother had always told her that she'd been gifted with a pair of lying eyes. She'd used those "lying eyes" to her advantage more than a few times. Deliberately, she blinked again. "What sound?"

Thump.

Thump.

She shrugged, feeling the heavy weight of his hands against her skin. "I don't hear anything." *Come on, Carl,* she thought, *come just a little closer.*

"Someone's out there," her captor said, pulling her away from the door and forcing her to step behind him in one swift move. He pulled the knife from his belt and reached for the doorknob.

"What are you doing?" She grabbed his arm. He couldn't go after Carl. Her neighbor was eighty years old! And this man, whoever he was, looked like he was in his mid-thirties. And he outweighed poor Carl by a good ninety pounds.

"Let me go." He shrugged her arm aside. "I have to protect you."

Her jaw dropped. "What?"

"Go to your room. Lock the door. I'll come for you when it's safe." His tone was fierce, like a commander who was used to giving orders. The knife glinted.

She sprang forward and blocked the door. She spread her arms out, grabbing the hard wooden frame. "Wait! Stop! That's my neighbor! You can't hurt him!"

"Sara?" It was Carl's voice, thin with fear. "Are you all right?"

The man before her blinked once, then slowly lowered his weapon. "You know him?"

"Yes."

The stranger closed his eyes a moment and inhaled deeply. "I don't sense evil from him."

"Uh, right. No evil there." Her gaze dropped to the glinting knife. If she could just get psycho-boy to put it down...

His eyes snapped open. "Psycho boy?" His face twisted. "Who is this psycho boy?"

How had he—

"Sara!" Carl was pounding on the door. "Sara, girl, can you hear me? Are you all right?"

No, she wasn't all right. There was a maniac with a knife in her living room, but if she screamed, he might attack Carl.

The maniac in question frowned and looked down at the knife. "I'm not going to hurt him. You can relax. And I'm not a maniac." His lips thinned as those strange silver eyes returned to rest on her face. "Neither am I 'psycho boy.'"

Oh, my God. Was he reading her thoughts? He couldn't be. That was impossible. That was—

He vanished. One moment, he was standing in front of her, nearly six foot three inches of intimidating muscle and man, and in the next instant, he was gone.

She screamed.

Her gaze flew frantically around the room. Where had he gone? Where was he? He had to be there—

"Sara!" Carl's voice was shaking. "I'm going to call the cops!"

She whipped around and jerked open the door. Carl stood on her porch, dressed in his customary black robe and red pajama bottoms. His right hand was clenched around the top of his cane. When he saw her, he jerked back in surprise.

Sara grabbed him, barely managing to stop him from falling onto the wooden porch.

"Carl, thank God!" She had met Carl right after she moved into the neighborhood three years ago. He had a habit of spying on his neighbors, and in that moment, she could have kissed him for being so nosy. "Someone's in my house!"

His brown eyes seemed to double in size. "What?"

Grabbing his arm, she quickly led him down the porch steps. "Come on, we've got to get out of here!" She glanced back over her shoulder, her gaze darting past the open front door. She couldn't see the man anymore, but she knew that he was still there.

She could *feel* him.

Don't run from me, Sara. His voice drifted through the night to her. *Don't be afraid of me. I'm here to protect you.*

"From what?" She asked, shaking her head dazedly.

Carl jumped at her voice and looked at her, his eyes still far too large for his face. "Girl, are you all right?"

Her heart nearly stopped. She knew she'd just heard the man's voice. She couldn't mistake that deep, rumbling voice. But he wasn't anywhere around. And Carl was looking at her like she was the crazy one...

"Did you hear him?" She whispered, clenching her fingers around his arm. "Did you just hear him?"

Carl shook his white head slowly.

She swallowed back the fear that rose in her throat.

Oh, my God...

* * * *

"The place is clear." The man in the blue uniform with the shining gold star stepped out of Sara's bedroom and headed down the hall. "Whoever your visitor was, he's long gone."

Actually, Torian le Fury was standing two feet away from the mortal. He'd used a simple cloaking spell to hide his presence.

"Are you sure about that, Mac?" Sara asked, her face appearing strained. "Did you check all the rooms?" Her hands were fisted and her lips were pressed into a thin line.

"Mac" stepped directly in front of Torian. The human was so close Torian could smell him and easily hear the sound of his breathing.

Mac lifted his hand and touched Sara's cheek. Every muscle in Torian's body tensed at the contact.

"Relax, Sara. There's no sign of your intruder. He's gone."

Torian didn't like seeing the other man's hand upon Sara's delicate flesh. No, he didn't like it at all. A low growl rumbled in his throat.

Sara's bright blue eyes widened and she jerked back, her gaze searching the room. "Did you hear that?" She whispered, lifting a hand to the pale column of her throat.

Mac frowned.

You heard nothing. There's nothing here. The house is safe. Torian issued the compulsion without a second's hesitation.

Mac slowly shook his head. "I didn't hear anything."

Torian smiled.

The sheriff seemed like a nice enough fellow, when he wasn't touching Sara, but Torian needed to get the man out of the house. He wanted to talk to Sara, to convince her that he wasn't a danger to her.

Torian knew that he'd handled things badly. He hadn't meant to scare Sara. Scaring her had been the last thing on his mind. He'd planned to make contact with her tomorrow. He'd thought he'd go down to her gallery and introduce himself in a normal, human way that wouldn't threaten her.

But he'd been drawn to her. As the darkness of the night had covered the city, he'd felt a strange stirring inside his body. A need. A need for her. And he hadn't been able to stay away. He'd had to see her. To smell her. To touch her…

Sara.

She was everything he'd hoped.

So beautiful. So pure.

She was small, barely reaching his shoulders. Her body was tiny, delicately proportioned. She had golden hair, a bright, shining mane that fell to her chin. Her skin was a pale porcelain, her complexion absolutely flawless.

She had large, beautiful blue eyes and a small, straight little nose. Her chin was slightly pointed, and her cheekbones were high slashes. Her heart-shaped face and delicate brows gave her an almost pixie-like look.

Of course, Saralynn Eden Myers wasn't a pixie. She was a witch. A hereditary witch with enough power in her small body to destroy the world.

And that was why Torian had crossed the dimension web to find her. To claim her. He needed Saralynn. He needed her power, her magic, and he would do whatever he had to do in order to possess her.

He was just lucky that he'd gotten to her first. The Dark Ones were also after her, and he couldn't, *wouldn't,* let them get their hands on her. He'd die first.

"Yeah, everything's clear." Mac was walking toward the door.

Sara followed on his heels. When she'd returned to the house, she'd pulled on a pair of faded jeans, but she hadn't bothered to put on shoes. Torian rather liked her small feet, and her hot pink toenails.

"Will you keep a patrol in the area, just in case that nutso comes back?" she asked.

Torian frowned at her.

Mac opened the door. "I'll get Quint to circle by. And if you see any sign of that guy again—"

"You'll know." Sara shook her head, and her short blond hair swung gently against her face. "If that creep comes back, I'll scream loud enough for the whole neighborhood to hear."

One corner of Mac's mouth hitched up. "You know, if you

get too scared, you could always come to my place." When
Sara just stared at him, he blinked innocently. "Hey, what are
friends for?"

A loud roaring seemed to fill Torian's head. The mortal
was actually flirting with Sara. The fool didn't know how close
he was to serious injury.

"I don't think friends are for *that,* Mac." Sara pushed him
over the threshold. "Good night."

"Ah, Sara." He put his hand over his chest. "You're breaking
my heart. Why, *why* do you torment me so?"

A laugh slipped past her lips. A light, musical laugh that
instantly captivated Torian.

Mac winked at her. "I'll see you later. Call me if you need
anything."

"Thanks."

Sara stood in the doorway a moment longer, and when the
policeman got into his car, she stepped back. Then she sighed
and shut the door. "You never change, Mac," she murmured,
rubbing the back of her neck.

Torian watched her as she carefully turned out the living
room lights and then padded into the kitchen. He realized that
he liked to watch her, liked to watch the expressions on her
face and the graceful movements of her body. She opened the
refrigerator and pulled out a carton of milk.

"Sara, we need to talk."

She jumped and spun around. The milk carton fell to the
floor and white liquid spilled across the tiles.

Sara's wide blue-eyed gaze swept around the kitchen. She
crept forward, not even appearing to notice the milk that coated
her colorful toes. "Who's there?"

Torian took a deep breath. Great, she was scared again. He
could almost smell her fear.

He didn't want her to fear him. He needed her to trust him,
to love him, not to fear him.

He waved his hand in front of his body, instantly making
himself visible.

Sara screamed, the sound deafening.

Two

"Don't be afraid." He held his hands up and took a tentative step forward. "I vow on my life that I won't hurt you. I'd never hurt you."

She stumbled away from him, her face white. "What the hell just happened? Where did you come from?"

"I've been here the entire time."

"No." She shook her head and pressed back against the countertop. "You weren't here. The kitchen was empty. One minute I'm alone, the next..." She swallowed, her gaze drifting over him. "The next, you're here."

"I was cloaking my presence." He lowered his hands. "I thought about teleporting out, but that uses too much magic."

"Wh-what?"

"Teleporting. It drains too much power." A little shrug. "I only port when it's an emergency."

What was he talking about?

"So I just cloaked, until that human male left." His lips curved down in apparent displeasure. "He stayed far too long with you. And there was no need for his presence. I would never harm you."

"Right." She squeezed her eyes tightly shut and then opened them. "Dammit, you're still here."

His lips thinned. "I'm staying until we talk."

"Jesus. Wait." His words finally registered in her mind. "What did you say you'd done? Cloaked? What the hell is cloaking?" She began to slide away from him, her back still pressed against the counter. Her feet made a soft squishing sound in the milk as she moved. Sara could feel her heart racing frantically in her chest. Her face was tingling and she was very, very much afraid that she would faint. And she'd never fainted before in her life. *Never.*

"I made myself invisible," he explained, his voice sounding strangely calm and clear. "I used a cloaking spell so that your sheriff wouldn't see me."

"And, uh, teleporting?" She was really almost too afraid to ask.

"That's when I can travel from place to place as easily as this." He snapped his fingers.

"Oh, God." Sara closed her eyes as she finally understood what was happening. "I'm having a nervous breakdown, aren't

I? You're not here. I'm imagining you. I'm imagining this whole conversation!"

"No, I'm real," the figment of her imagination said in a deep, husky voice.

She lifted her lashes. "Well, at least if I'm crazy, I'm fantasizing about hot men."

He blinked once and a dull flush stained his high cheekbones.

"I'm glad you find me...appealing," he said slowly. "That will make things easier."

Wait a minute. Did imaginary men blush? Sara forced herself to let go of the countertop and take a step toward him. She reached forward—

And touched him. She felt the cold leather of his jacket beneath her palm. She moved her hand, and she could feel the tight muscles of his chest. Could feel his heart beating, pounding faster and faster beneath her fingers.

Oh, my God. "You're real," she whispered, her hand pressed against his chest.

He nodded, his silver stare taking on a heated, sensual look. His right hand lifted and captured her wrist, forcing her to press her palm harder against him, forcing her to feel the strength of his muscles beneath her fingers. "I'm real," he whispered, bending his head toward hers.

And for just a moment, all she could think about was feeling his lips against hers. She wanted to kiss him, to taste him. She wanted him to taste *her*.

Maybe she really was crazy.

"I've been waiting for you for so long," he whispered, and his lips captured hers.

She thought about pushing him away. She thought about elbowing him in the ribs or kneeing him in the groin. Then his tongue stroked against her lips and she could only think of how good he felt.

His mouth stroked hers. Caressed. His tongue thrust against her lips, slid into her mouth. And, damn, but she liked the way he kissed. Liked the press of lips, the swirl of his tongue. His big hands came up and framed her face, tilting her to better receive his kiss.

She could feel the force of his desire pressing against her. Strong. Hard.

Her hips rubbed against his. God, she needed to touch him, needed to—

She jerked back, her eyes widening. What the hell was she doing? She was letting him put his hands all over her. Worse, she was putting her hands all over him!

"Let me go," she gritted, struggling to slip free of him. He held her tight, his hands clenching around her arms.

His silver gaze seemed to burn brighter. A dull flush coated his cheekbones. "But you want me. I felt your desire."

Yeah, and she'd certainly felt his. Her stomach clenched. "What I want is for you to let me go." She pulled against him, and was startled by the unbreakable feel of his hold. A lick of fear shot through her. "Let me go *now.*" It was an effort to keep her voice steady. But she could not, *would not,* let him know that she was afraid.

He held her stare for a moment longer. Then his jaw clenched and his hands fell away.

She immediately jumped away from him. She paced quickly around the room, deliberately putting the small kitchen table between them.

He watched her, his eyes brooding. And he made no effort to hide the arousal pressing so solidly against the front of his formfitting pants.

He studied her in silence, his stare unnerving. After a few moments, he shook his head. "You're not what I expected."

She blinked. "What?"

"Not that I'm disappointed," he murmured, his gaze dropping to survey her body. "In fact...I'm quite pleased with you."

Great. Fabulous. He was pleased. "Who the hell are you?" she snapped. "And why are you in my house?"

One black brow shot up. "Oh, sorry. I should have introduced myself sooner." He bowed elegantly, his coat swirling around him. "My name is Torian le Fury."

"Le Who?"

His lips thinned. "Le Fury."

"Uh, okay." Her gaze slid to the back door. Ten feet. Could she distract Mr. Fury long enough to sprint that distance?

"No, you can't." He sighed. "And it's le Fury, not Mr. Fury."

Sara actually felt her heart stop beating. Then it began pounding again in double time. "Who are you?" *What are you?* And how the heck was he reading her mind?

"I told you." He shrugged, looking slightly offended. "But for some reason, you seem to be having trouble with my name."

She blinked. And then she pinched herself. Hard. "Ouch!"

He was beside her in a flash. He took her right arm in his warm, strong hands, and surveyed the red flesh with a critical eye. His brows drew together as he turned to study her. "Why would you do that?"

Oh, lord, she could smell him. A rich, masculine scent that wrapped around her.

He tapped against her wrist. "Sara?"

She swallowed. "I'd hoped I was dreaming." His fingers rubbed against her and goose bumps rose on her arm. "Guess not."

"No, you're not dreaming." He continued to stroke her wrist. "I'm quite real."

Okay. So there was a very real, very large man in her kitchen. Her gaze lowered to his belt and the gleaming knife that hung near his waist. *Correction*, a very real, very large, very *armed* man in her kitchen.

And he appeared to have the power to read her mind.

"Are you sure this isn't a nightmare?" she whispered. She'd eaten a whole lot of chocolate candy bars before bedtime. And she distinctly remembered watching some show about monsters...

"No." There was an edge to his voice now. She could almost hear the impatience.

Sara exhaled. She'd said it before, but..."I want you to leave." Now.

"I can't do that." His gaze locked with hers. "You're in danger."

Yeah, from the big guy with the knife.

"No, I'm here to protect you."

She jerked her hand free. "Stop doing that! I don't know where you come from, Fury, but around here, we don't poke into other people's heads!" Having him know all her thoughts was seriously annoying. And more than a bit scary.

He flushed. "I apologize, but you're broadcasting."

She gasped. "I most certainly am not!" She didn't really know what broadcasting was, but she was dang well not doing it.

"Yes, you are." His lips pursed. "Perhaps if you tried shielding your thoughts."

"Shielding my..." She closed her eyes and counted to ten. Then she looked at the man in front of her. "Look, buddy, I haven't the faintest idea of what you're talking about."

His muscles tensed. "You don't know how to shield? But

even children can close their minds to others!"

She walked away from him, trying to keep her movements casual and nonthreatening. "Yeah, well, good for them, but I can't shield my thoughts. I wouldn't even know how to try."

"Then we've much work to do," he said with determination. "Don't worry, I'll teach you."

"Right." She was almost to the door now. "Look...ah..." What was his name?

His gaze lit with anger. "Torian," he gritted.

She smiled at him, a huge, guileless smile. "Right, sorry." She cleared her throat. "Ahem. You know...Torian...you still haven't told me why you're here." *Why he'd broken into her house in the middle of the night.*

"I had to come," he said simply. "You're in danger."

"From...you?"

He shook his dark head. "No. From the Dark Ones."

It just got weirder and weirder.

"They will take you," Torian told her, his tone low and intense. "They will use your power—"

"Yeah." She grimaced. "Here's the thing. I don't really have any power to take."

His hands fisted at his side. "You do not believe me."

Wow, maybe there was hope for tall, dark, and deranged after all. She tried to carefully choose her words. "Let's just say that I think you might have the wrong house." Yes, that sounded diplomatic enough.

He took a step toward her. "I am where I should be." A pause. "You are the woman that I seek, Saralynn."

Saralynn. A shiver slid over her. Only her mother had called her Saralynn. And her mother had been dead for thirteen years. She lifted her chin. "I want you to leave."

"The Dark Ones will come. They will take you."

"Leave." Her jaw clenched. "Now." She pointed toward the kitchen door. Could the guy not take a hint?

He walked across the room, but he didn't head for the door. He stopped in front of her. "You bear the mark of the witch."

What?

"It sends off energy. Powerful energy. It will draw them." He lifted his hand to touch her cheek, but she flinched away from him.

"Look, I don't have any mark." She looked him straight in the eye as she spoke. "There's some mistake here. You and these Dark Ones have the wrong woman—"

He stepped closer. She could actually feel the heat of his body. "You are the one I seek."

"No, I'm—"

His eyes narrowed. "I'll prove it!" He reached for her shirt and yanked the garment up, exposing her midriff.

"What are you doing?" she yelled, struggling against him. "Stop!"

His hands wrapped around her, his fingers locking against her hips. He unsnapped the top of her pants, pushing them down to ride low on her hips. He stared down at her exposed flesh, satisfaction on his face. "There."

"There? There what?" Sara glanced down at her stomach. There was nothing to see. Sure, she had in her customary gold hoop belly button ring, but other than that...

He pointed to her right side. "You bear the sign."

She squinted. He was pointing at her faint pink birthmark. "Uh, I hate to disillusion you, Fury, but that's called a birthmark."

He looked up at her. "Have you never noticed its shape?" His thumb stroked against the faint mark.

His touch felt so warm. And there were calluses on his hands, as if he spent a lot of time working outside. His hands were big, strong, but his touch was featherlight.

"Have you?" he pressed. "Have you noticed its shape?

What? She blinked and slowly shook her head. She barely paid any attention to the mark.

"It's shaped like a sword."

"Really?" She glanced down, frowning. "Hmmm...are you sure about that?" She couldn't really tell from this angle, but it looked more like an airplane to her.

"All witches of the High Family have that mark, for they are the designated protectors of their people." His fingers closed over the birthmark, as if to hide it. "The Dark Ones will sense the sword, and they will come for you."

"I really don't think—"

"You'd better accept what I'm telling you before it's too late."

Too late? Too late for what?

He glanced toward the window. Faint streaks of light slipped through the blinds. "The dawn comes. The Dark Ones cannot hunt during the day. The sunlight saps their strength."

"Uh...good."

"You'll be safe until nightfall."

"Okay." The way she figured, it, she'd be safe once Fury got out of her house.

His lips thinned. "I must leave, but I will return to you as soon as I can."

"Take your time," she murmured. "No rush."

Fury's jaw clenched. "You will accept what I have told you as truth, or you will pay the penalty."

"The penalty? And what's that?"

"You'll forfeit your life." He stepped back, bowed to her and then calmly walked out of her back door.

One. Two. Thr—Sara lunged forward and threw the lock. Then she stood on tiptoes and peeked out of the nearby window, trying to see where Fury had gone. Where he'd—

Her backyard was empty. The man had vanished..

She blinked. He'd done it again. The man had disappeared. Into. Thin. Air.

"Damn," she muttered softly, raising her hand to rub against her birthmark. This was starting to look bad. Very bad.

Because if Fury wasn't just some figment of her imagination or some crazy magician...

Then she could be in serious trouble.

You'll forfeit your life.

Sara shivered.

* * * *

He'd probably scared her to death, Torian realized. *Good.*

Saralynn needed to be afraid. She needed to be absolutely terrified. Because the Dark Ones wouldn't stop until they had her.

He'd returned to the mountains, returned to the cabin he'd found nestled far from prying eyes. He settled in, making certain the curtains were carefully drawn across the small windows.

Sara.

She hadn't been what he'd expected. He'd thought he would a find a woman already prepared for the fate that awaited her. A woman trained in his ways. A woman who knew her role.

He didn't think that Sara really knew anything about what was going on. Pity. Her ignorance could get her killed.

His fingers curled into a fist as he remembered touching her, touching the bare skin of her stomach. She'd felt so soft, so warm. And he'd wanted to strip all of the clothes from her delectable little body and spread her out on her kitchen table...

But it wasn't time for that yet. Later. Later, he would have his fill of Saralynn. After all, it had been foretold long ago. She would belong to him. She would be the mate that he'd sought for ages.

She would be his mate forever. And she would give him her power. The power of a full High Witch.

He smiled. Soon. The time would come soon.

But first, he had to protect his lady. He wasn't going to let the Dark Ones or anyone else hurt a hair on her blond head.

He closed his eyes and prepared for the deep sleep that he knew would come. After sliding through the dimension web, sleep would hit him hard. It always did.

But Sara should be safe while he slept. The Dark Ones only hunted at night.

He felt his heart slow down, felt his body become heavier, heavier...

And the last thing he saw before the darkness covered his mind was her.

Sara.

* * * *

The sun was just beginning to sink beneath the horizon when Sara left the art gallery. She'd planned to be out of The Artist's Dream by five, but Zack, the idiot manager that she was truly growing to detest, had made her stay late to catalog a new shipment of art.

Art. She snorted. There was no way that crap she'd just spent two hours reviewing was "art." Her five year old neighbor could do a better job. The artist had basically just cut the labels off of soup cans and glued them to a canvas. Then he'd called it "Breakfast." And there was a whole series to go along with "Breakfast." And they were all just as bad.

Of course, Zack thought they were brilliant. Since he was the manager and she was the lowly assistant manager, they'd had to go by his opinion.

Even though the man was an idiot.

She growled low in her throat and locked the front door to the gallery. She'd set the security code moments before, so the place was locked up tight.

Glancing around, Sara was surprised to see that the normally busy area was empty. Usually, there were shoppers milling around or couples walking hand in hand down the cobblestone street.

Anders, Virginia, was a quaint tourist town. It was one of those places tucked away in the middle of absolutely nowhere. A secret spot. The perfect place to get away from it all.

She loved Anders. She loved the quiet nights. The small-town feel. After living the first sixteen years of her life in Chicago, Anders had been a welcome change for her.

She turned away from the door and pulled her coat closer to her body. She needed to hurry home. She'd promised Carl that she'd feed his cat. Carl had left at lunch time to go visit his brother in Charleston, and he wouldn't be back in town until early next week. The sweet old guy had actually called her and offered to cancel his trip because of the "scare" she'd had last night. But she'd told him she was fine, that he should go ahead and have a great time with his family. And, of course, that she'd take care of Lola.

Yeah, she needed to hurry home so that—

"Sara..."

She jerked to a stop. The hair on the nape of her neck stood up. Her eyes searched the street, but she saw no one.

A soft laugh echoed down the lane. *"I see you, Sara..."*

The voice was high, almost childlike, and it sent fear coursing through her.

She turned slowly, her gaze sweeping over all the buildings, over all the shadows. She could feel someone watching her, could actually feel the gaze as it rested on her body, but she saw no one.

She took a tentative step back. Then another.

The laughter followed her.

"W-who's there?" She knew it wasn't Fury. She would have recognized his deep, rumbling voice. But if it wasn't Fury, then who—

"I've been searching for you." A man stepped out of the shadows. He was dressed all in black. His face was very pale. Too pale. And his eyes seemed to glow red.

Oh, God. Sara stood frozen, her gaze trapped by that red stare.

He smiled and appeared to float toward her. "I knew I would find you first," he said in that childlike voice. "I knew..."

She blinked, forcing herself to look away from his eyes. She glanced down at his feet. And...Jesus...he *was* actually floating. She wet her lips. "You're not, by any chance, a-a Dark One, are you?"

His smile widened, and she saw that his teeth were very sharp. Too sharp. They were like an animal's.

Screw this. She turned and ran. She wasn't going to waste time trying to fight that...that *thing*. She was getting the hell out of here. The sound of his screams chased her down the street.

"You're mine, Sara. Mine! Mine! Mine!"

Her heart was thudding frantically against her breast, her legs were burning, and she didn't really care what the crazy thing behind her was saying. She just wanted to get as far away from him as she could.

Dammit, where were all the people? Why was the street deserted? It was *never* deserted.

She glanced back over her shoulder. He was trailing her, barely twenty feet away. His arms were reaching out, his fingers extending toward her, and she could see that his nails were like claws.

"Help!" she screamed, turning back around. "Somebody help me!" *I'm being chased by a bogeyman and I think he's going to eat me.*

Then she remembered Fury's words. *You'll forfeit your life.* Damn, she should have listened to him. He'd tried to warn her, but she'd dismissed him as being crazy. *Fury.* She needed him. He could help her. He could—

A man stepped out of an alleyway and, startled, she ran straight into him.

She expected to fall. She expected them both to tumble onto the unforgiving cement. Instead, he twisted his body and grabbed her, holding tightly to her before she could stumble. His leather coat swirled around them.

"Hello, Saralynn." Fury smiled down at her. "You didn't have to run to seek me out. I would have come to you."

She was so thrilled to see him that she threw her arms around him and held onto him with all her strength. He stiffened against her. Then his arms lifted and wrapped around her body, holding her against him.

"Fury!" His name was a shriek of rage.

He lifted his head and looked at the creature before them with disgust. "You're the one they sent?" He shook his head. "Please, this won't even be worth the time it will take for me to kill you."

The creature screamed, a loud, piercing sound. The sound ripped straight through Sara. She gasped in pain, her hands lifting to cover her ears.

Fury just shook his head. Then he pulled a black pouch out of his jacket.

Sara looked back at the creature, feeling that horrifying

scream reverberate through her entire body. Damn. It hurt so much.

The creature kept screaming, but its eyes widened in sudden fear.

"You'll never have her," Fury snapped, and threw the pouch.

White powder spilled through the air and onto the creature, and just that quickly, the screaming stopped. The man, or whatever he was, vanished.

She blinked. Her hands were still covering her ears. She was afraid to move them, afraid that the horrible screaming would start again.

Torian wrapped his fingers around her arms and pulled gently. "It's all right now. He's gone."

She blinked. A faint plume of smoke drifted from the spot where the man had stood. "G-gone?" Her brows drew together. "Gone where?"

Torian's look was unflinching. "You don't really want to know that."

She gulped and her knees buckled. Torian caught her before she fell, scooping her up into his strong arms and cradling her against his chest.

"I'm not Buffy," she murmured. "I can't handle this stuff."

His brow lifted. "Who is this Buffy?"

She closed her eyes and rubbed her cheek against his chest. She could smell the leather of his jacket and hear his heart pounding. "Her TV show's over, but she slayed vampires."

"Oh." His arms tightened around her. "Then it's good you're not her. I don't need you to kill vampires."

Well, that was something at least.

Torian began walking down the street. She decided she should really make some sort of protest. After all, she was no lightweight. She didn't want him throwing his back out because he was carrying her through the streets. "You can put me down. I can walk." Even to her own ears, her voice didn't sound convincing.

"Umm...true." He turned the corner and kept a fierce hold on her. "But I like the feel of you in my arms."

And she liked being there. Liked being wrapped in the scent of leather and man. Liked the feel of his strong arms around her. She felt safe. Protected.

"I guess I should thank you," she whispered.

"Yes," he said seriously, "you should."

She frowned.

He walked toward a black SUV, opened the passenger door and placed her carefully on the seat. She was surprised. The man tended to disappear on her with the blink of an eye. She hadn't been expecting him to be driving around the city in a new model sport utility vehicle. "Is this yours?"

He glanced at her as he slid into the driver's seat. One dark eyebrow arched. "What do you think?"

She looked around at the spotless interior. She could smell the distinct new car scent. "I think you just stole this thing off a car lot." Great. She was about to drive off in a hot vehicle.

His mouth hitched into a half-smile. "Relax. It's not stolen." He cranked the engine. "It's mine…for the time that I'm here."

He pulled onto the road.

"You know, I probably shouldn't be here with you." She kept her gaze on his strong profile as he drove. "My grandparents always told me to watch out for strange men." And Torian definitely qualified as strange.

"You're safe with me," he assured her. "You have nothing to fear."

Other than being attacked by some creature with red eyes, claws, and abnormally sharp teeth. She sighed. "Somehow, I just don't believe that." She pointed toward the upcoming traffic light. "Turn here. My house is two blocks down."

"I know."

Her eyes narrowed. Of course. The guy had broken into her place last night. It figured that he'd mapped out exactly how to get to Meadow Street.

"I'm sorry I didn't meet you at the gallery," he said. "I'd planned to be there long before the Dark One arrived."

Her hand lifted to her side, rubbing against her birthmark as a sudden fear stirred within her. "Did I really draw him to me?"

Fury nodded.

"But why? I mean, I'm twenty-nine years old. If I were some kind of…of Dark One magnet, wouldn't they have swarmed me by now?"

"No, your Becoming is at hand. They wouldn't have sensed you until now."

"Excuse me? My what is at hand?"

His jaw tightened. "Were you told nothing of our ways?"

He sounded annoyed. And that made *her* annoyed. "Look, Fury, I don't know anything about 'our ways.'"

The vehicle turned into her driveway. Fury stopped the car

and turned to face her, his gaze brooding. "Did your mother not tell you—"

"Whoa!" She held up her hand and realized that fingers were trembling. "My mother's been dead for thirteen years. It's not like she's had the opportunity to tell me much of anything."

"What?" He shook his head. "She was to prepare you—"

She fumbled with the door handle. "Yeah, well, she didn't get to prepare me for much, okay? A drunk driver hit her on Christmas Eve." Actually, the driver had hit them. She'd been in the car with her mother at the time. They'd been on their way home from the church Christmas pageant. The blue pickup had appeared, as if from nowhere, and plowed straight into the driver's side of her mother's sedan. Sometimes, late at night, she could still hear the sound of her mother's screams.

"Sara." Torian was touching her, rubbing her arm. "I'm sorry, Sara. I didn't know."

She shrugged his touch away and finally managed to shove open the door. "Forget it." She sprang from the SUV and hurried up the porch steps.

"I cannot forget it. You are in pain." His words seemed to echo through her head.

She looked back at him. He stood in the middle of her walkway, gazing solemnly back at her, and she realized that he hadn't said anything just then. Not out loud anyway. Suddenly enraged, she turned on him. "Stop doing that!"

He blinked.

"Stop messing with my mind! I don't want you poking around in there, okay?" Her thoughts were her own, and she didn't want Fury eavesdropping in her head.

He drew himself up stiffly. "Fine."

"Fine? What does that mean?"

Fury's lips tightened, and he gritted, "It means I won't go into your mind again without your permission. Unless I have to."

Unless I have to. Well, it was better than nothing. "Good." Her porch light shone faintly, illuminating the circle of space just before her door. She spun around, intending to go inside and lock Fury out as quickly as she could, but she stopped and drew in a deep breath. Then she turned back to face him.

He stood as before, all but motionless on her stone walkway. His features were tense with some unnamed emotion.

"I'm sorry," she said, her voice soft. "It's just...my

mom…she's a soft spot for me. I-I can't talk about her." Not
with anyone. It just hurts too much.

He nodded.

There was a strange lump in her throat and her eyes were
stinging. Great. In another moment, she'd probably break down
and cry in front of him. "Um, thanks for taking care of that guy
for me." Guy. Scary demon. Whatever he'd been. "And, uh,
thanks for seeing me home." She dug into her pocket and pulled
out her keys. "If you hadn't been there, I would have had to
walk home." She glanced past him to the dark night and
swallowed. "Normally, I drive my car, but it's in the shop. I
thought a quick walk home would be all right. I was supposed
to be out of the gallery before it was dark." Because she hated
the dark. Always had. But then that idiot Zack had kept her
late, and she'd walked outside only to discover that the daylight
was gone. And that the growing darkness was waiting.

"It would not have been safe." His silver eyes glinted. "The
night is no longer safe for you, Sara."

"Um, right." Her fingers curled around the keys. "Well, I
guess I'd better go in."

He shook his head and took a step toward her. "I don't
think you understand what's happening."

Well, no, she didn't. She understood that some sort of weird
creature called a Dark One had tried to attack her. And she
understood that her mother was supposed to have prepared her
for the "Becoming." But other than that, she was pretty clueless.

All things considered, though, she was actually kinda proud
of herself. She wasn't screaming hysterically or anything. And
most people, if they were nearly attacked by a creature with
red eyes and fangs, would probably be in the middle of a
breakdown by this point.

"You're right," she finally said. "I don't understand a damn
thing that's going on." And she wished, really wished, that it
was all just a very bad dream. She looked at him, cocking a
hand on her hip in a deliberately belligerent pose. "Wanna fill
me in?"

"Sure." He stalked slowly up the stairs. "You're not like
other women, Sara."

Hey, wasn't that what she'd always dreamed a man would
say to her? That she was different? That she was special? It
was a pity her ex-husband had never gotten around to saying
stuff like that to her.

"I bet you say that to all the girls," she muttered.

The stairs creaked beneath him. "No," he said, his voice deliberate. "I don't." His stare was trained on her, and it was heated. Almost...hungry.

Her heart began to race. "And how am I...different?" Lord, the man really was something. She could see the strength in his body, see it in the ripple of his muscles. And she could see the lustful warmth in his eyes.

And for a moment, she was so very tempted to touch him. To caress him. To lean forward and taste him.

He reached out and cupped her cheek in his hand. He tilted her head back, forcing her to look deep into his eyes. Her breath caught. Had he read her mind again? Was he about to kiss her?

Because she wanted him to kiss her quite badly. She wanted to feel his lips against hers. Wanted to feel the strong thrust of his tongue. Wanted to taste him.

"Torian..." Was that husky, needy voice really hers? It couldn't be.

His gaze dropped to her lips and she thought he was going to do it. Thought he was going to kiss her again. And she wanted his kiss, wanted him...

He pulled back, cocking one dark brow. "How are you different?" he repeated, as if mulling over the question.

She blinked, realizing she'd all but forgotten their conversation. What had they been talking about? Sara frowned, thinking. Oh, yeah. She cleared her throat. "Um, I'm not...different, you know."

"Yes, you are different. Very different." His stroked her cheek. "You're not who, or rather *what* you think you are."

Come again? She squinted up at him, feeling completely lost. "I have no idea what you're talking about."

A sigh lifted his broad shoulders. "I know, and that's half the problem." His stare was intense. "To begin with, you're not a mortal. You're a witch."

Three

Torian watched as Sara's sexy little bow of a mouth dropped open in shock.

"I'm a what?" She squeaked.

He fought the curve of his lips. "A witch."

"Oh, no." She was vigorously shaking her head and backing away from him. "No way. I don't dance naked in the moonlight. I don't ride a broom or turn people into toads—"

"Umm." He rubbed his chin. "Would you like to?"

Her face blanched. "No!"

Pity. He rather liked the idea of Sara stripping down and dancing under the light of a full moon. Of course, she'd get to do that during the Becoming. And as for the toads...well, that was child's play for any High Witch.

Sara's face flushed a light pink. "And, look, I don't even have a cat. Aren't all witches supposed to have cats?"

Meow. A large Siamese cat padded onto the porch. She paused for a moment and then walked toward Sara. Her long white tail curved around Sara's calf.

Torian looked at Sara, arching one brow.

"Don't look at me like that," she snapped. "She is *not* my cat. She's Carl's cat." She glowered at the animal. "And she's just here because she knows I'm supposed to feed her."

"Ummm." He rubbed the bridge of his nose.

Sara's blue eyes narrowed. "She's not my—my...Oh, what do they call them?"

"Familiar?" he supplied helpfully.

Sara snapped her fingers together. "Right! She's not my familiar, and I—" She paused, pointing to her chest. "I am not a witch!"

He crept closer to her, deliberately crowding her against the front door. He inhaled her scent, a light, sensual fragrance that clung to her skin. "Yes," he said softly, enjoying the way her eyes widened and her lips parted. "You are."

She shook her head. "No, I'm—"

"Your mother was a witch," he told her. "And you've got her talent." His gaze dropped to her waist. "And you've got the mark."

Her body slumped against the door. "Tell me this isn't happening."

He stroked her arm. Because he had to touch her. Had to feel her soft skin. "I can't do that." He lifted his head and his gaze scanned across the darkened neighborhood. It really wasn't safe for them to be outside. Ember, the Dark One that he'd dispatched in the street, had been very weak. He'd almost been too easy to kill.

The Dark Ones were obviously sending out scouts to search for Sara. When word reached them that *he* was with her, they would send their best fighters after him.

Luckily, he'd dusted Ember before the Dark One had a chance to send out a warning message to the others. That should buy them some time. Not much, but some.

"We need to get inside," he murmured.

She nodded, turned and quickly opened the door. The cat ran inside ahead of her, purring loudly. Sara grimaced. "I'd better go feed her."

"Go." He nodded. "I'll make certain the doors and windows are safe." A quick protection spell should do the trick for the time being.

She shrugged and scooped up the cat. "Come on, Lola. Let's get you some grub." Her high-heeled shoes rapped softly against the wood as she walked. "And you are so not my familiar," Sara muttered, just before disappearing into the kitchen.

Torian lifted his arms and closed his eyes. He called forth the power from within and began to chant. Ancient words. Powerful words. Words that humans could never comprehend. Words that had been bred into his very soul from the beginning of his existence.

He was aware of the change in the air. Aware of the soft touch of a cool wind on his skin. The hair on his nape stood up in response to the sudden electric charge in the room.

He opened is eyes. He stared at her front door. Torian pointed his hand toward the door. Blue sparks shot from his fingertips.

"Oh, my God!" Sara stood a few feet away from him. Her blue eyes were huge. "What the hell are you doing?"

Very slowly, he turned his head to look at her. He knew she would see the glow in his silver stare.

Stumbling back a step, Sara raised a hand as if to ward him off. "Better question," she whispered, her breath coming in quick pants. "What the hell are you?"

He sent the magic from his fingertips in a quick burst. Blue electricity zapped around the house as the spell took effect and secured the windows and doors. No Dark One would be allowed entrance to Sara's home. They would be safe this night.

"Ah, Torian?" Sara was starting to inch back down the hallway.

Closing his eyes, he fought to dispel the lingering power from his gaze. He didn't want to look at her again, not with the burning fire reflected in his eyes. "Give me a moment."

Silence.

He cracked open one eye. Sara was tiptoeing down the hall as fast as she could. In another few seconds, she would be into the kitchen, and then, no doubt, running out the back door. Torian sighed. He really hadn't wanted it to come to this, but if she kept fighting him, kept denying what she was seeing...

He lifted his hand and blue fire shot toward her.

She screamed and then froze as blue bands formed around her body.

He motioned to her, crooking his finger. The blue bands lifted her into the air and pulled her toward him.

All of the color bled from Sara's face. Torian swore. He knew he was terrifying her, but he had to make her realize what was happening. She couldn't keep fighting him. And she could not, absolutely *could not,* run from him.

She belonged to him. There was no way he'd let her escape.

With a wave of his hand, Torian made the blue bands disappear. Sara stood before him, barely two feet away. Close enough that he could reach out and touch her if he wanted.

And he did want to touch her. He wanted to smooth her brow. To pull her into his arms and tell her that everything was all right.

But he couldn't do that. Not yet. Because he had to force Sara to see the truth of his nature...and of her own.

"I'm not like other men," he told her, and he knew that a shimmering glow would still be lurking in his gaze.

Her small pink tongue snaked out and licked her lower lip. "Yeah, I, uh, figured that out when I saw the blue lights." Her brow furrowed. "Let me guess. You're a witch." Sara's chin was in the air, but her voice was trembling.

"No." He shook his head. "I'm a wizard." The power that he had, the magic that he possessed, he'd fought for—he'd killed for. But Sara didn't need to know that, not yet. Torian stared at her, waiting for her response.

****

Oh, hell. Sara tried to breathe slowly and deeply. And she tried very hard not to start screaming like a mad woman. But...damn, a wizard?

Her gaze traveled slowly over Torian's body. He was wearing his black leather coat again. And those tight, form fitting pants. He had on his tall, black boots, the boots that looked like something a pirate might wear. Dangerous. Sexy.

And, of course, he still had that extremely large knife strapped to his belt.

"No offense," she murmured, "but you don't really look like a wizard." Weren't wizards supposed to be old, white-haired men who wore blue hats with stars on them?

"Oh, and have you seen many wizards, dear Sara?"

She flushed. Okay. So the only wizards she'd seen had been on television. "No."

He shrugged. "We come in all shapes...and sizes."

She waved a hand toward the den. "So that blue light business...that was just you...doing wizard stuff?"

His jaw flexed. And his gaze smoldered. "That was me protecting you." He paused. "Because you don't have the power to protect yourself."

Her entire body stiffened. "Now wait a minute—"

"You're an untrained witch," he snapped. "You couldn't protect yourself from a baby troll, much less a Dark One."

A baby *what?*

"You're like a newborn." His gaze swept over her and his expression hardened. "Completely defenseless."

"I am not defen—" She took an angry step toward him.

The blue bands immediately reappeared, locking tightly around her. She realized that she couldn't move a single muscle.

He smiled, a dark, taunting smile. "Don't you understand, yet? I'm not human. Neither are the creatures that are after you. We don't play by your rules. And we can do things to you—" The bars tightened a fraction. "—that you can't even comprehend."

She tried to speak, tried to open her mouth, but she found she had no voice.

Torian stepped closer and stroked her cheek. "Poor Sara. I didn't want it to be this way. But you wouldn't listen. You just kept denying what I said to you. Denying what you saw."

She wasn't denying anything anymore. She was terrified. He'd trapped her with nothing more than a wave of his hand. And she was helpless. Completely helpless. She couldn't move. Couldn't speak.

It was just like before, when she'd been trapped in the car. She'd watched her mother slowly bleed to death, drop by precious drop, and the blood had coated the floorboard. Had pooled at her feet.

Oh, God. She was trapped. Her mother was dying—

"No!" Her scream echoed only in her mind. Her rage, her grief, burned in the cry.

Torian staggered back, clutching his head between his hands as he fell to his knees.

The blue bands disappeared.

Sara stood there, breathing raggedly, as the past slowly disappeared.

"Damn," he muttered, rising slowly. "You pack a hell of a punch."

She rubbed her arms. Where had the bands gone? "What?"

He rubbed his temple. "I wasn't going to hurt you, you know. I just wanted you to understand." He winced. "Damn. I wasn't expecting you to be so strong, not without training."

What was he talking about now? She frowned, realizing that faint white lines bracketed his mouth, and his eyes looked...strained. "Torian?" Something was wrong. Sara bit her lip, realizing she actually felt pain emanating from him. "What happened?"

"What happened?" He repeated, blinking. "You happened."

Huh?

He pointed toward her with a hand that shook slightly. "You sent me a wave of pure pain, and it almost knocked me on my ass."

She blinked, remembering the terror-filled scream that had filled her mind. She'd been trapped in the past, and she'd desperately wanted to be free from her memories. There had been so much pain there, so much heartache. She'd just wanted to escape the pain...

"So you threw it at me," he murmured, studying her with his head cocked to the side.

A frown pulled down her brows. "You said you'd stop doing that," she reminded him, tensing slightly.

"Yeah, well, these aren't exactly normal circumstances."

He closed his eyes and winced again. "I wasn't expecting you to attack me."

"And I wasn't expecting you to—to—" To what? Tie her up? Trap her in blue bonds of magic?

"I had to do it," he said simply, opening his eyes. "I had to convince you that I was telling the truth."

Her knees seemed to give way beneath her, and Sara sat down on the couch. Hard. "I don't need any more convincing." She swallowed, trying to ease the sudden dryness in her throat. "I know everything you've said has to be true." There was no other explanation. The Dark One who'd come after her and then vanished. The blue beams of light. The way Torian could apparently appear and disappear at will.

It was real. All of it. It wasn't some dream. Some nightmare. It was real.

Magic.

There were creatures out there, hunting her. Creatures that wanted her power. Power that she hadn't even known she possessed.

She looked up at Torian, at the strong lines of his body, and she knew that she needed him. Needed him desperately. Because she didn't think that she could protect herself. Not from the creatures that were coming.

"Help me," she whispered, hating the weak sound of her voice. Hating that she had to ask *anyone* for help. She could usually handle everything on her own. But this was far beyond her experience. "Please." Oh, God, she was begging.

He crouched before her. The white lines of pain were already fading from his face. "I was sent here to protect you. I won't let anything hurt you." He lifted his right hand and pulled back the sleeve of his coat, revealing his wrist where a faint tattoo marred the skin.

"What's that?" She could see the design of the black ink, see the sharp edges that looked like—

"It's a shield." He held out his wrist. "It marks me as a Guardian."

"A Guardian?" She frowned down at the black etching. "What's a Guardian do?"

"Protect witches."

Sara looked up at him.

"There aren't many of you left," he said simply. "The Dark Ones have hunted witches almost to extinction."

Oh, that was not good. Definitely. Not. Good. "Why do they hunt witches?"

"Because they steal their power." He took her hands in his. "Just like they'll steal your power if they get the chance."

Her power. Just what kind of power did she have? And what would happen to her if those *things* actually succeeded in taking it from her?

"I was sent here to keep you safe until the time of your Becoming."

Yeah, he'd mentioned that before. Her head was starting to pound. And she really didn't know if she liked the sound of a "Becoming." Just what, exactly, would she become, anyway?

"We don't have much time," he was saying, as she stared blankly at him and wondered if her body was going to transform and become some entirely new creature. "I have to take you back—"

"Whoa!" Sara interrupted, holding up her hand as she instantly snapped back to attention. "Take me back? Back where?" She hadn't agreed to go anywhere with Fury.

"To my world."

Oh, my. "Um, this…isn't your world?"

A quick shake of his head.

Oh, my. He wanted to take her somewhere. To a different world. "Please tell me it's not 'in a galaxy far, far away.'"

He frowned at her, and Sara suddenly wished she wasn't sitting on the couch. Wished that he wasn't kneeling in front of her, with his big body caging her against the cushions.

"Taren is on the other side of the dimension web."

Dimension web. Right. She swallowed. "And just how does one cross this web?" Not that she wanted to do that.

"You need a passage spell in order to get back to Taren. The spell burns a lot of energy, so after the web walk, your magic is weaker for a few hours."

Taren. "What's your…world like?" The question slipped out, spurred by her curiosity.

He sighed softly, and his breath stirred the hair against her cheek. "A lot like Earth. For ages, wizards and witches have crossed the web, traveling back and forth between the worlds. We learned from humans, and humans—often unknowingly— learned from us. Our languages are the same. Clothing. Food. Inventions. All the same. Well, except for technology." A faint frown appeared between his brows.

"What's wrong with technology?" As far as she was concerned, technology was pretty freaking amazing. She loved being able to cook her dinner in less than five minutes. Loved programming her VCR to catch all her favorite shows.

"Technology weakens magic." His eyes narrowed. "So we use it as little as possible. The electrical impulses in the air actually change when cars and computers and cell phones are used, and those impulses can dampen a wizard's power."

"Yeah, well, I can see where you wouldn't want that," she muttered. But damn, no microwave? No computer? No email? His world wasn't sounding all that great to her.

"The magic is still strong in my world. But here—" Torian paused, shaking his head. "Here, everyone's forgotten the magic, turned away from it." He smiled. "On Taren, the magic is as powerful as it was in the beginning."

"The beginning?" Oh, damn, why did she keep asking him questions? Because his answers were just making her feel worse.

"When all the realms were created." A pause. "My world, your world, heaven, hell…"

Her hand lifted, stopping him. "Look, Torian, this is really a lot to take in." Dark Ones. Other worlds. Magic. She really wasn't up to learning anymore right then. Sara tried to push against him, to rise, but he wouldn't move, wouldn't let her off the couch. She swallowed. "And you know, I'm kinda happy here. In this world, that is. I mean, my boss is a jerk, and I haven't had a date in a year." She flushed, realizing she was probably revealing a bit too much information. "But, it is *my* world, and I don't want to leave."

His jaw tightened. "You don't have a choice." He slid her knees apart and inched between her spread thighs. He was so close she could feel the heat emanating from his body. "If you stay here, you'll die." His gaze smoldered. "And I can't let that happen."

If you stay here, you'll die. "Torian—"

"My *world* will die," he said, his heated gaze moving to rest on her lips.

"What?"

A muscle flexed along his jaw. "The Dark Ones have almost taken over Taren. If you don't come back with me, if you don't help me fight them…"

Now she had to *fight* the Dark Ones? She shook her head. "I can't! I saw that—that *thing.* I couldn't fight it!" And as far as going to Taren, well, that just scared the crap out of her. Going to another world was not her idea of a good time.

"I'll teach you," he said softly. "I'll teach you everything. I'll train you. Prepare you for the Becoming."

Hmm…There was that word again. The "Becoming."

"Yes, um…" My, it was hard to concentrate when he stared at her like he was hungry and she was his meal. She shivered. "Um…what is…a Becoming?"

He slid his hand down the curve of her neck. The leather of his jacket rubbed against her breasts, and a strange heat bloomed low in her belly.

"It's happening already," he whispered, lowering his head toward hers. "Don't you feel it?"

Her heart was racing. Her hands were damp.

He slid his hand down two more inches. His fingers cupped the curve of her breast. She wanted to arch into his touch, to rub against him.

His left hand locked around her waist and he pulled her forward, sliding her hips to the edge of the couch. He was on his knees before her, with his body firmly wedged between her spread legs. He thrust his hips against the juncture of her thighs, letting her feel the strength of his arousal.

"I can smell you." His voice was little more than a growl. "Your scent is calling to me. Your time is close. So close."

Sara felt hot, achy. She wanted to press her body against his. Wanted to feel him against her, *in* her. Buried deep. Thrusting…

"It's so close," he whispered, bending to lick her throat. "I can taste it on your skin. The power…"

Oh, God. The muscles of her stomach clenched, and she had to bite her lip to hold back the moan that rose in her throat. Her fingers fumbled, pushing aside his jacket. She grabbed his belt, trying to pull it loose.

"No, Sara. We can't." His gaze was burning now. "Not yet."

She didn't hear him. She could only hear the roar filling her ears. Could only feel the desire sweeping over her.

She'd never felt like this before. Never wanted anyone this badly. She had to have Torian. Had to be with him. Had to feel him thrusting, hard and deep, into the depths of her body.

Her hands slid along the front of his pants, and she cradled his thick length, feeling him jerk against her. "Torian…"

He shuddered. Blue sparks filled the air.

Her clothes felt too tight. Too confining. She wanted to strip them off. To be naked. Completely naked. Skin to skin with him.

His hands clamped around her questing fingers. His gaze, molten silver, trapped hers. A dull flush stained his cheekbones. "It's not yet time, Sara."

She twisted, trying to get free. Needing to touch him.

"Sara!"

She blinked, the sharpness of his tone pulling her from the strange sensual haze that had surrounded her. She looked down, horrified to see that her fingers were still stroking him.

Panting, she jerked her hand away from him. Need still twisted through her, but her control was back. For the moment. "What the hell was *that?*" She eyed him suspiciously. Had he put some sort of sexual spell on her? Because there was no way, absolutely no way, she had done that on her own. Her ex-husband had told her that she was frigid. He'd said she was a dull lay, and that was why he'd started an affair with his secretary.

That twisting, moaning, needful woman that she'd been just moments before…that wasn't her. That was *not* Sara Myers.

"Your time is close," he said again, rising to tower over her.

"My time?" She shook her head. "Dammit, Torian, I have no idea what you're talking about!" She pushed to her feet, pausing a moment as she realized that her thighs were trembling.

He inhaled, and his body seemed to tremble. "I can smell you," he whispered.

She sniffed delicately. She didn't smell a damn thing. What was the man talking about now? And why did he even care about her smell? They'd almost made love less than ten seconds ago. Couldn't the man focus on the important issue?

His hands tightened into fists. "Your need is driving me crazy."

Her need? She stiffened.

He took four quick steps away from her. She noticed that his body was tense, his muscles straining, and she really, really wanted to touch him again. She curled her fingers, feeling her nails bite into her palms.

"It's the Becoming." He was across the room now, regarding her with a stern stare. "You're readying—"

Her head snapped up. Readying? She didn't like the sound of that. "What...is...the...Becoming?" She gritted.

For an instant, his control slipped, and she saw a flash of ferocious hunger in his gaze.

"Torian?" She took a step back, almost frightened by the lust that was etched so clearly on his face.

He shuddered. "It's a...ceremony."

Her eyes narrowed. "What kind of ceremony?"

His gaze swept over her body, lingering for a moment on the tight peaks of her breasts. "A mating ceremony."

"*A what?*"

"Your body is readying, preparing for the ceremony."

Her body was readying? Her eyes widened in horror. She remembered how she'd felt moments ago. Remembered the flood of desire that had burned through her. Remembered how she'd rubbed herself against Torian's powerful body. Rubbed herself against him like a cat in...

"Oh, my God!" She shook her head.

His gaze was on her breasts again, and she could feel her nipples swelling. She wanted him to touch her again. Wanted him to...

"Ah!" She spun around, folding her arms over her breasts. This was bad. Very bad. Because unless she missed her guess, she was...in heat. Or something very close to it.

"It's the way of our people," Torian growled.

She turned to face him, deliberately keeping her breasts shielded from his view. "I'm not one of your...your people." And dammit, she felt like some kind of animal! And she *wasn't* some mindless animal seeking sex.

"Yes, you are." He swallowed, and she noticed that his eyes were no longer that molten silver. He looked calmer, more in control.

She wished she felt the same way.

"You're going to mate soon," he told her. "When the Becoming is upon you, you'll mate. Your powers will come to you, full force, at that time."

She didn't like the sound of that. Her apprehension must have shown because Torian sighed softly.

"It's natural," he said, his voice strangely soothing. "The woman's body prepares for her mate. She readies. Her scent..."

She stiffened. He'd mentioned her scent before. "What about my scent?"

"It calls to the wizards. It lets them know your time is at hand."

She flinched. Just great. According to him, she was in some kind of weird heat, and her scent was attracting wizards.

And her birthmark was attracting Dark Ones.

"You will mate soon," he continued, "and your power will sweep through you."

"What if I don't want...to mate?"

He stared at her. "You will."

And she knew that he was right. Moments before, her body had been on fire. She'd wanted to make love with him right then, right there, on her grandmother's old couch.

"This isn't me," she whispered, feeling shame rush through her. "I'm not like this." She'd only been with one man her entire life, and making love with her husband, well, she'd never particularly enjoyed it. He'd only touched her in the dark. And he'd been fast, almost rough. "I don't just...have sex...with strange men."

"Good." His lips tightened. "Because I don't share my mate. Not with anyone."

He didn't... She gulped. "Wait a minute! I am *not* your mate."

Blue sparks danced around him. Oh, man, what was up with the sparks? He'd better not be getting ready to put a spell on her.

Torian smiled slowly, and the sparks seemed to flare brighter. "You will be."

Four

When Sara's brilliant blue gaze widened in horror, Torian realized that he'd made a mistake. But it was too late to take back the words.

She needed to get used to the idea of being his mate. Before the week was out, she would belong to him. And their joining would last forever.

"I am not going to m-mate with you!" She tilted her head back, sticking her cute little nose straight up in the air.

"Yes, you will." Their fates had been predestined. There was nothing either of them could do to change their future. Besides, Torian didn't want to change his destiny. He wanted Sara. Wanted her for his mate.

And he would have her.

Even if his mate-to-be was currently stomping around the room, her lovely features twisted into a ferocious scowl.

"Let me get this straight," she muttered, pivoting sharply on her heel as she paced back toward him. "There are monsters after me. I'm about to start acting like a cat in heat, and I'm supposed to have sex with you?"

"No," he corrected her, making an effort to keep his voice calm and even. "You're going to mate with me." Mating was different from sex. Sex was fleeting. It fulfilled a temporary need. Mating was forever. But he didn't point that fact out to Sara. The woman looked far too stressed as it was. If he told her that their mating would link them forever, well, she'd probably try to run from him again.

Her shoulders slumped. "I thought you said you were here to protect me." She sounded strangely lost, and from the moment he'd met her, she'd appeared so strong. He felt his heart tighten, and he took a step toward her, unable to help himself.

"I am." He was sworn to protect her.

"Then why—"

The house started shaking. A loud boom echoed from just outside. And the sound of maniacal laughter seemed to slither through the house's very walls.

Sara closed her eyes. "Don't tell me." Her tongue slipped out and licked a quick path across her lower lip. "It's another Dark One, right?" Her eyes opened slowly.

He nodded. Then he stepped forward, grabbing her arm.

"Stay behind me. Whatever happens, stay right with me." Damn. He wished he could just transport Sara back to his world, but he knew if he tried to do that, she'd flip. She wasn't ready to go to Taren, not yet. And if he forced her now, she'd never trust him.

And he needed her trust. Had to have it.

Without her trust, she'd never give him the power he sought.

"A-all right."

Torian hummed softly, sending a questing wave of magic out into the night. He needed to know what he was facing. How many foes were waiting on him.

Sara tapped him on the shoulder. "Um, I know you're doing your blue light thing and all, but, uh, weren't you supposed to have secured the house earlier?"

A picture fell off her wall. The floor shook beneath them.

He glanced back at her, scowling.

She blinked. "What? I thought you'd taken care of this."

"They're not inside, are they?" Torian snapped. "I just made sure no one could get in. I didn't make certain the house couldn't be destroyed." Which appeared to be exactly what the creatures outside were doing. Board by board, they were ripping the house apart.

A loud crack sounded from directly overhead. The sound of breaking glass echoed in the distance. The cat yowled.

Sara grabbed his elbow. "Look, he can't destroy my house! This house belonged to my grandmother. I *love* this house."

A large crevice started to appear on the far wall.

She pulled harder on his elbow. "Dammit, Torian, stop him!"

"Let go of me, and I will!" Couldn't the woman see that he was concentrating? If she would just give him a minute... He turned around, giving her a quick glare.

Her hand fell away. She frowned back at him, her brows lowered quellingly.

He sighed and glanced back toward the front of the house. Closing his eyes, Torian summoned his power.

There were two of them outside. Rage was riding them hard. He could feel the dark emotion swirling around them. They knew that Sara was inside. They'd sensed her mark.

He slipped into their minds, easily reading their thoughts, their evil plans. They wanted to take Sara. To hurt her. To steal her powers.

They sensed the Becoming. They wanted to use her, to—
His gaze snapped open. *Change of plans.* "Stay here."

For once, she didn't argue, and he walked toward the door.
It swung open instantly at his approach. He began chanting as
he crossed the threshold, calling up the power of the elements.
Calling fire to him, calling wind.

The Dark Ones screamed as he approached. The scream of
a Dark One had been known to fully incapacitate a man. It
could paralyze, freeze nerves, and shatter bones.

The screams had no affect on him. They usually didn't on
wizards, but they could kill witches.

He hoped that Sara was shielded by his spell. He didn't
want her to be in pain, to be trapped by the screams.

The Dark Ones didn't immediately attack him. Their white
bodies looked almost transparent. With a glance, he could tell
that they were young, recently transformed. They wouldn't have
the power of time on their sides. But they would still have the
strength of young wizards.

For only a wizard could be transformed by the Dark. Only
a wizard could trade his natural magic for the strength of the
night. And the power of the night…it was so tempting to many.
The dark power of the night could double a wizard's strength.
Some even said it could give a wizard immortality. But in truth,
it was a deadly trade. For in return for the Dark strength, a
wizard would lose his very soul.

Once the dark trade was made, a wizard could no longer
tell the difference between right and wrong. Hell, the wizard
no longer *cared*. The hunger for more power was all that the
Dark Ones knew. In order to get that power, they attacked
witches. And they were even starting to hunt Guardians.

The two Dark Ones were circling him now, raising their
arms. He knew they were preparing a merge spell, knew they
thought that their combined strength would be enough to defeat
him.

But they were wrong.

The wind began to howl and a streak of blue flame shot
across the lawn. Torian smiled as the power flowed through
him. So strong. So pure. There was nothing like the feel of
magic. Nothing.

The wind ripped against the Dark Ones. Their long hoods
fell back and their clothes billowed. The fire raced toward them,
the hungry flames heading straight for their bodies.

In just a few more moments, the battle would be over. They would be dead.

The screaming ended, and the figures slid back several feet, their cloaks swirling around them.

"We just want the woman, wizard," one of them said, his voice soft, almost purring. "Give her to us, and we'll let you walk away."

"I'm not giving you the woman." He paused. "And I'm still going to walk away." He focused the fire and sent a strong pulse of energy toward the Dark Ones. "But you won't."

The flames streaked toward them.

The Dark Ones didn't stay to fight any longer. With a shrill cry, they disappeared, fleeing before the force of the flames. His lip curved in disgust. *Cowards.*

The door squeaked behind him. He turned just in time to see Sara poke her head outside.

She glanced around, lifting a blond brow. "Where'd the bogeymen go?"

To lick their wounds. "They ran." But they'd be back, and next time, he would make certain that he finished them off.

Her gaze drifted over her still-smoking lawn. Flames flickered near her wooden fence. "Uh, yeah. I would have run, too." She cleared her throat. "None of my neighbors…saw this, did they? Cause it would really be hard to explain how you were out here fighting bogeymen with fire."

"They aren't bogeymen," he said, waving his hand to eliminate the signs of battle. "They're Dark Ones."

"Whatever." She stepped onto the porch, rubbing her arms as if she were chilled. "I just don't want them to come back."

But they would be back. They would keep coming, keep trying to take her. And he couldn't allow that.

"We have to leave," he said, knowing they would have to act fast. There was much to do before the Becoming. Much he had to teach Sara. Much that she had to experience.

She was shaking her head. "No, Fury. Look, we already covered this, remember? I told you, I like my world. I don't want to leave."

His jaw clenched. "They're going to come back. They'll bring reinforcements."

Her chin lifted. "Then I'll just find a way to fight them." A deliberate pause. "I thought I did a pretty good job of fighting you earlier."

He remembered the blast of pain she'd sent at him, literally sending him to his knees. Yes, she did have power, but she didn't have *control* of her power. She wouldn't be able to use it effectively against the Dark Ones. Not yet.

"You're not strong enough to fight them now. They'd rip you apart," he told her, knowing the words were harsh. But there was no choice. He couldn't, *wouldn't,* allow her to risk her life.

She paled at his announcement.

"Now, come on, Sara. We don't have much time."

Her arms folded across her chest. "For the last time, I'm not going!"

Torian launched himself up on the porch and grabbed her. "They'll kill you!"

"I'm not going to leave my home!"

He jerked her toward him. The porch light shone down on her. He could see the faint gold flecks in her gaze, could see the smooth beauty of her skin. And the fierce determination on her face.

"Sara…" He knew it would be hard for her. She would be leaving the life, the friends, she'd known. The world he'd show her would be far different from this one.

"No." She shook her head quickly. "I'm not going. Find somebody else."

Damn. This was going to be harder than he'd thought. But there really was no choice. He had to protect her. "I'm sorry," he whispered. "I hope you can understand."

Her eyes widened. "Understand what?"

He didn't answer. He reached up and stroked her cheek. Her skin was so warm. So soft. His gaze fell to his lips. Such perfect red, full lips. And he remembered how she'd tasted.

His head lowered toward her. He needed to kiss her again, just one more time. Torian expected her to pull away. To fight him.

Instead she met him, her lips parting instantly for the thrust of his tongue. His arms wrapped around her as he pulled her close. His mouth fed on hers. God, she tasted like sweet wine.

His tongue slid deep into the warmth of her mouth. He couldn't get enough of her. Had to have more.

Torian fought for his control. Now wasn't the time. He couldn't have her. Not yet.

Slowly, so slowly, he lifted his head, breathing heavily.

She stared up at him, her mouth swollen from his kisses.

Sara wet her lips. "That…doesn't change…anything." Her chin lifted. "I'm not…going anywhere…with you."

Her pulse pounded furiously at the base of her throat. Torian could see the faint tremors that shook her body. He stroked her shoulders. "Sara…I don't remember giving you a choice."

Her mouth dropped open in surprise, and he grabbed her, lifting her in one quick move and hoisting her over his shoulder.

"What the hell are you doing?" Her voice was a screech, and her fists pounded against his back. "Let me go!"

"No." *Never.* He wouldn't leave her here. She would be a sitting duck.

She hit him again, a particularly hard punch that lanced across his back. He grunted.

"Put…me…down." The words were gritted from between her teeth.

He turned and walked carefully down the old steps. The cat screeched and shot past him, disappearing into the nearby trees. Torian's SUV was waiting for them just a few feet away. His arm tightened around Sara's knees when she tried to twist her body off his shoulder. "Stop it, Sara! I'm not letting you go."

"You can't do this! It's kidnapping!"

He yanked open the passenger door and eased her down onto the seat. She immediately tried to lunge out of the car. He grabbed her, pressing her back against the leather. "Stop it!"

"No!" She screamed. "I'm not going with you!"

"And I told you, you don't have a choice." He stared deep into her eyes and linked with her. *I have to do this. There's truly no choice, not for either of us* He thought about using the magical bonds on her again, but he hesitated. She'd been able to defeat that spell, been able to send that blast of pain to counteract his power. He'd better try another trick with her this time…

Her hands trembled against him. "Get out of my head."

I'm sorry. He knew what he had to do now, but he hated to force a compulsion on her.

"Don't be sorry," she snapped. "Just let me go!"

I can't. He took a deep breath. *Close your eyes, Sara.*

"What?" She twisted, struggling. "You close your eyes, jerk!"

Close your eyes. And breathe. Deep. Feel the sleep calling you.

She blinked, her struggles easing. "I-I don't…"

Sleep. You're safe. Just sleep. It would be easier to transport her if she wasn't fighting him.

Her lids lowered. He could still feel the tautness of her body and knew she was trying to fight him. But he also knew that the power of his compulsion would overwhelm her. She simply wasn't strong enough to fight him. Not yet.

Sleep.

Her head slumped forward. "B-bastard," she whispered. Then her eyes closed.

Torian pulled her against his chest, holding her tight for just a moment. He could feel the steady beat of her heart. Could smell her light, sweet scent.

And he knew that she was right. He was a bastard. But he wasn't letting her go.

* * * *

Sara's lashes lifted slowly. *Damn. What in the hell had happened to her?*

She blinked against the bright light, and the room shifted into focus. And she saw…him.

Torian was leaning over her, a faint frown between his dark brows. The man was stark naked.

She jerked upright and screamed. Her memory came flooding back to her.

Torian shot out of the bed. His muscles tensed and his gaze searched the room. "What is it? Where's the danger?"

Sara kept her stare locked on his face. She *would not* drop her gaze and peek at his…

"Sara!" His hands were on his hips. His hair, free of its tie, hung loosely around his strong face. "Where's the danger?"

Standing right in front of her. "You're naked," she told him, her voice hushed.

He blinked, then glanced down at his body. His shoulders lifted in a shrug, and his expression clearly said, *So what?*

"And you were in bed with me," she continued, her fingers clenching around the sheets.

"You're going to be my mate," he said, stepping toward her. "I plan to spend a great deal of my time in bed with you." He reached for the covers.

"Stop!" She wasn't going to let him crawl into bed with her. The jerk had put some kind of whammy on her, kidnapped her, and gotten in bed with her. And, oh, yeah, she could just guess what he wanted to do next...

His jaw tightened.

"Where am I?" Oh, Lord, she hoped she wasn't in the "other world" that he'd talked about. *Taren.* Because if he'd taken her to some other dimension...

He crossed his hands across his chest and glowered at her. She glowered right back.

Torian's lips twitched. "You know, you're really beautiful when you're angry...and in my bed." His hands dropped to his sides.

And her gaze dropped with them.

Oh, Lord. She blinked. The man was seriously aroused. His erection was long and thick, easily wider than her wrist. The dark head stretched toward her—

Her gaze snapped back up to his face, and she found him watching her, a knowing gleam in his eyes.

"See something you like?" he murmured. "Because I certainly do."

With a small effort, she managed to swallow. The man was...impressive, to say the least. "Ahem." She took a breath. Better get back to the matter at hand.

He slid onto the bed, and his thigh brushed against hers. She tensed. "What are you doing?"

His fingers stroked her arm. "Relax, Sara. I don't bite."

Yeah, right. "You kidnapped me," she reminded him with a sharp glare. "You knocked me out."

"No, I didn't. I just sent you to sleep, for a little while."

Her back teeth clenched. "You knocked me out," she repeated. All she remembered was hearing his voice. It had sounded so soothing. So tempting.

"I put you to sleep because you left me no choice." There was no remorse in his tone or his gaze. "As my mate, I must put your welfare first in all things."

"I'm not your mate!" When would he drop this damn mate thing?

"Yes, you are." He inhaled deeply, sliding an inch closer to her. "Your words deny me, but your body calls to mine. I can smell you now. Your scent, your need. You want to be with me."

"What I *want,* is to go home." But she didn't meet his eyes as she spoke, because while she wanted to deny it, there was a part of her that wanted him. Wanted to stroke the hard muscles

of his chest. Wanted to trail her hand down the steely expanse
of his stomach. Down, on down, to his groin. To touch, to stroke,
the heat of his arousal.

His nostrils flared, and his eyes flashed a silver fire.

"I know what you want," he whispered. *"I know."* He lifted
his hand and rubbed it down her arm, the tips of his fingers
brushing against her breast. She sucked in a quick breath.

"I wanted to undress you," he whispered, "while you slept.
I wanted to strip the clothes off you and touch all that smooth,
pale skin."

Oh, boy. A wave of heat swept through her. The idea of
him stripping the clothes from her body, of him seeing her,
touching her, left her aching deep inside.

"It's the way of our people," he said, his fingers stroking
lightly against the curve of her breast. "We sleep body to body.
Chest to chest. Mates exchange power that way. We bond."

His touch felt so good. A moan rose in her throat. She
wanted to arch into his touch. Wanted to kick away the sheet,
wanted to strip off her clothes and feel him, as he'd said, *body
to body, chest to chest.* "D-don't." Oh, but his touch felt so
good.

His fingers stopped.

She looked at him, meeting his bright stare.

"I have every right to touch you," he gritted. "You've been
marked for me since the moment of your birth. You're mine,
Sara. *Mine."*

She shook her head. "I don't belong to you. I belong to
myself." She scrambled from the bed. Damn. Why did her body
have to be so damn responsive to him? She wished that she
wasn't aching for his touch. Yearning, for him.

"Sara…"

She didn't look back at him. She didn't trust herself to do
so. There was a door to her left. Her bare feet padded across the
wooden floor. The floor was slightly cold and the touch of the
old wood chilled her toes.

Sara reached for the knob, wanting to get away from him,
needing a moment to get her control back, to think.

Pushing the door open, she saw that a gleaming bathroom
waited before her. She hurried inside, locking the door behind
her. Her heart was racing, and she could still see him in her
mind. See his body…and she kept imagining what it would be
like if they made love.

"Get a grip," she whispered, gazing in the mirror at her slightly flushed reflection. "The man kidnapped you for heaven's sake!"

"Only because I had to," Torian said, his voice soft.

"Jesus!" She spun around, her hand lifting automatically to cover her heart. He stood in the doorway, hands crossed over his chest. "Can't you knock?" Apparently locks didn't work so well with wizards.

His dark brows pulled together in a frown.

"Don't sneak up on me like that!" The man moved like some kind of cat. And he was too damned big to move that way. He should make some kind of sound. That way, she wouldn't become humiliated when he walked up and caught her talking to herself.

"I had to take you from that house." His head bowed. "I know you don't want to be here, but I have to keep you safe."

"I was safe there." Okay, maybe that wasn't entirely true. She'd been safe until the bogeymen showed up at her door. After that...well, things had gotten a little dicey.

She was vastly relieved to see that he'd pulled on a pair of pants. Of course, the man looked very good in said pants. *Too* good and too damn tempting by far.

The man's a kidnapper. Don't let his sexy smile and tight abs distract you!

She took a breath and tried to regain her focus. "Where are we anyway?" she snapped, pushing past him. So much for getting time to think.

"My cabin."

She glanced around the room, noticing for the first time the rich mahogany walls. "And where might this cabin of yours be located?" *Please, please don't tell me it's in another world.*

"In the mountains, about two hours away from Anders."

Oh, that was good. Some of the tension eased from her shoulders. "How is it that you have a cabin, anyway? Aren't you supposed to be an all powerful wizard? Why do you need some place in the woods?"

"Because I need a safe place to train you," he said simply. "I have to prepare you for the Becoming, and it was too dangerous to stay in Anders."

She walked toward a small window. Glancing through it, she saw a vast stretch of land. Tall pine trees, arching mountains. Blue skies. "And this place isn't dangerous?" Honestly, it didn't look dangerous. It looked like some kind of postcard. She slowly turned back to face Torian, turned away from the beautiful view.

"This is ancient land. Spells of protection have been here for centuries." His gaze narrowed, as if in thought. "The Dark Ones won't be able to come here."

That was even better. She really didn't want to see another Dark One. Ever.

Her ears still ached from hearing the first evil creature's scream.

"There's much I have to teach you. Much to show you."

Uh oh. Was he talking about the Becoming again? Her gaze slid to the front of his pants. She rather thought he'd already "shown" her plenty. And, Lord knows, she'd certainly gotten an eyeful.

"Maybe that's not such a good idea," she murmured.

His lips tightened. "The full moon rises in less than a week." A pause. "On the fifteenth."

The fifteenth. Her eyes widened. Her thirtieth birthday was on the fifteenth!

"You must be ready by then," he continued. "Your power will be at full force. You must be able to control it, to control yourself."

"And if I can't?" What would happen if she couldn't handle this great power that he kept talking about?

He shook his head. "That's not an option." His stare was hard, and a shiver slid over her. "You *will* handle the power. I'll make certain of it."

A really bad feeling was growing in the pit of her stomach. "But what will happen if I can't handle the power?" She wasn't going to let this drop. She needed to know.

His jaw clenched.

"Fury, tell me."

He exhaled on a heavy sigh. "You'll destroy both worlds, yours and mine."

Oh, damn.

He stepped toward her and cupped her chin. "But that's not going to happen."

Apparently, the man did not know her well. She pretty much failed at everything she did in life. When she'd turned sixteen, it had taken her seven tries just to get her driver's license. She'd flunked out of three different colleges. She'd had over a dozen jobs. And her marriage had ended in less than two months.

She did *not* have a good track record with success. Damn. This was not going to be good.

"Can you just find someone else?" She whispered. "Give the Becoming to another woman?"

His fingers stroked her skin. "You *are* the only woman. You are the last of your line."

Her line. A line of witches. "Are you telling me that my mother…?"

"Was a High Witch?" he finished for her. "Yes, she was. She fell in love with a mortal and she gave up her world to come and be with him." A pause. "With you."

"They were happy," she said, remembering. "They used to laugh all the time." They'd held hands when they walked. Kissed every time they saw one another. Yes, they'd been so happy. Their lives had seemed perfect until her father had gotten sick. Cancer, the doctors had said. It'd spread through his body like wildfire. He'd died just six months before the accident that had taken her mother's life. And then she had moved to Anders to live with her grandparents.

"Mom was so lost when my dad passed away," she whispered, remembering. "She would just sit for hours and cry." It had been as if her mother had entered her own realm, and no matter how hard Sara had tried, she just hadn't been able to reach her. Not until… "She got better. Right before the accident." For a time, her mother's smile had returned and she'd seemed almost happy again.

She shut her eyes and wished that she could shut out the past as easily.

"This isn't going to work," Sara said, her voice still soft. Her lashes lifted and she stared at him. "I can't do what you want me to do." She wasn't strong enough to fight evil. Hell, she wasn't even strong enough to face her own memories.

"Yes, you can."

A quick shake of her head. "You don't know me, Torian. You don't know what I'm like."

"Yes, I do." He touched her temple. "I've been inside you. I've seen your thoughts, your past. I've seen all your secrets. *I know you.*"

She shivered. Suddenly, she felt too exposed. Naked. And she didn't like that feeling. She didn't like him knowing her pain. Her memories. Everything. She was bare before him.

"I don't remember inviting you in." But she distinctly

remembered telling him to keep the hell out.

"It's the right of a mate to know his woman. Inside and out." He didn't look repentant. He just appeared to be stating a fact.

Mate. The word slipped through her mind. Was she really meant to be this man's mate? "I don't want you in my mind," she told him, lifting her chin.

"I know."

"And I don't want to be a, a—" Oh, hell, what had he called it? "A High Witch."

"I know." Torian stepped away from her.

Of course he knew, because he knew everything about her.

"But I will," she told him, coming to a sudden decision. Her voice was a faint thread of sound as she said, "I'll do it." Yeah, she might be scared spitless by the idea, but she was going to try.

He watched her, his silver stare unblinking.

"*I'll do it*," she repeated, stiffening her shoulders. And she would not, absolutely *would not,* destroy the world in the process.

He eyed her with a hint of suspicion in his gaze. "Why the sudden turnaround, Sara?"

She remembered her mother's smile. Her mother's love. And her mother's last terror-filled moments of life. Her mother had begged Sara for help, but Sara had been trapped herself, and she'd just been able to stroke her mother's hand and watch her die. "Because I owe it to somebody." If that other world he kept talking about, if that place was really where her mother had come from, then she couldn't just sit back and let it die. And she sure as hell couldn't let *her* world die. She tilted her head back. "That's all I'm going to tell you." She was tired of him knowing so much about her. And he'd damn well better not sneak into her head again and try to read her thoughts.

"Then we should get started." He motioned toward the small den. "Come."

Her brows drew together. "What are we going to do?" Now that she'd committed to her training, Sara knew there was no going back. But that knowledge didn't stop the trickle of fear that shot through her.

"Oh, it's very simple." His hand pushed lightly against her back. "We're going to unleash your magic."

Five

Torian watched Sara arch one golden brow. "You're going to teach me to be a witch?"

"No," he said, and took a step toward her. He liked to be close to her, liked to inhale her scent. *Roses.* The woman always smelled just like roses. "I'm going to show you how to use the powers of a witch." He sighed. "Sara, you're *already* a witch; you were born that way. Your powers are just dormant. But we're going to wake them up."

"Is this going to involve flying on a broomstick?"

Her voice was mocking, but he answered her in all seriousness. "Yes."

Her lips parted on a breath of surprise.

"But that'll come later." Taking her hand, he marveled for a moment at the feel of her soft skin against his, and then he pulled her in front of the fireplace. A large chunk of wood sat just inside on a metal grate. "First, you've got to master fire."

"Fire?" she parroted, and her blue eyes lit with interest. "I get to make fire?"

She looked so damn cute. It was all he could do not to lean forward and kiss that excited smile right off her face. But, of course, if he started kissing her, there was no guarantee that he'd actually be able to stop. Not with the Becoming so close, readying her body, tempting him.

And every damn time that he touched her, he lost a little more of his control. He could hardly wait to claim her as his mate.

He'd almost given up hope of finding a mate of his own. The witches had all but disappeared, and while a wizard could have sex with a mortal, he could only bond with one of his own kind. And he could only sire children with one of magic blood.

With someone like Sara.

He hadn't known of her existence. Hadn't known that she was on her own, alone. If he'd known, he would have never waited to seek her out.

But a prophet had learned of Sara's existence only a few short weeks ago. And the prophet had come to him and said that his mate had—*finally*—been found.

And now she stood within his grasp. The Becoming was just days away, but he honestly didn't know if he could wait that long to claim her because he wanted her so badly. Wanted to touch every smooth inch of her body. Wanted to kiss her. To lick her skin. Her breasts. Her pink nipples. He wanted to spread her pale thighs and slide deep into her waiting warmth.

He just didn't know if he was going to be able to wait. But if he took her before the Becoming, he would be risking so much. He wouldn't be able to fully claim her magic. And he needed her magic, needed it to fight the Dark Ones that would come for them.

If he took her now, then he wouldn't be able to control her power, not once the full moon rose. But if he waited, if he could just manage to hold on to his damn control—a control that was growing dangerously weak—then he could use her power. Channel it.

He needed her power, needed it desperately if the Guardians were to win the battle against the Dark Ones.

But, damn, he *wanted* her.

"Uh, Fury?" Sara's soft voice broke into his thoughts. She was staring at the wood with a perplexed expression on her face. "Look, I've been thinking, 'fire, fire, fire,' but not a damn thing is happening here."

His lips twitched and a strange warmth slipped through him. "Sara, if it were that easy, don't you think everyone would be doing it?"

Her answer was a sheepish shrug.

He wrapped his arms around her and pulled her against him. Her back pressed against his chest and her legs brushed against his thighs.

"W-what are you doing?" Her voice seemed sharper, and he caught a quick whiff of the heady scent of her arousal.

His body tightened in immediate response. He clenched his teeth, holding onto his self control with all of his strength. "You have to relax," he whispered, breathing the words against her neck. Her scent was stronger there. Richer. *Sweet roses.* He wanted to put his mouth on her skin, wanted to see if she tasted as good as she smelled.

"Relaxing is a little hard at the moment," she muttered, holding herself stiffly against him.

His hands were on her hips, and he fought the urge to pull her back a few more inches, to rub his body against her and let her feel his arousal. Except now wasn't the time for mating. But soon...

"Close your eyes," he told her, his voice gruffer than he'd intended, but need was riding him hard.

"Why?" Now she sounded suspicious, but she *often* sounded suspicious. Of course, considering all that had happened, she had good reason for her concern.

"Because you have to concentrate. And when you're just standing there glaring at the wood, you can't concentrate." Conjuring fire took a strong will. Fire was thought to be the easiest of the elements to control, but, in truth, it took enormous strength because fire, if not properly controlled, could overwhelm a witch.

"All right." She exhaled. "I'm closing my eyes."

He shifted her body against his, turning her just slightly so he could peer down into her face. He nodded, satisfied. Her incredibly long lashes were lowered. "Good."

He sent his mind out, questing gently.

Her lashes snapped up. "What the hell are you doing?"

He kept his expression blank. Damn, but she was strong. He should have been able to cloak his presence, but she was already becoming attuned to him. Good. They would need that link later.

"I want you out of my head, Fury." Her voice was hard, cold. "How many times do I have to tell you—"

Yeah, he knew she didn't want to let him inside. But…"We have to link, Sara. You can't touch your powers until we do." Her magic was locked deep inside her mind, and she wasn't going to be able to pull forth her power unless she let him help her. She was going to have to trust him, because he would have to open her mind completely in order to free her powers.

He felt her flinch. "I-I don't know about this."

His fingers tightened around her slender hips. "Sara, I promise it will be painless." He knew she was afraid he would have power over her once he slipped inside her mind. But she needed him. She wouldn't be able to reach her core of magic alone. She'd lived in the mortal realm far too long.

Besides, he'd already been inside her mind. Seen her thoughts. Heard the whisper of her dreams. And it sure as hell hadn't given him any power over her. If it had, he wouldn't have had to kidnap his mate.

He felt her take a deep breath. Then she nodded. "Do it."

Elation roared through him at her invitation, grudging though it was. He focused his energy, thought only of her, and sent his magic questing into her mind.

She was stiff in his arms, and the moment he touched her thoughts, he could feel her withdrawal.

Sara. It's all right. You don't need to be afraid.

He felt her hesitation. Then, *I don't like this.*

Torian stilled. He could feel her voice sliding over him, through him, though she hadn't spoken a single word aloud. She was using their link. Using their bond to communicate.

You'll get used it, he promised her, sliding a bit deeper into the swirling realm of her thoughts. *It's the way of our people.*

Your people, she corrected him. *My people open their mouths and talk when they want to say something. They don't try some kind of Vulcan mind meld on others.*

Vulcan mind meld? What the hell was that?

He could feel the draw of her power now, sense it in her very essence. There was so much power there. Calling to him. Calling to be set free.

He could almost touch it.

Torian?

So close. The power was reaching out to him now, sensing him. Sensing its freedom. He'd never felt anything like it before. It was as if all of her magic were locked behind some sort of door, and all he had to do was open the door. Just open it.

Torian, I feel funny. Something's wrong.

No, everything was just right. She had more magical strength than he'd ever imagined, ever dreamed. He would use that power. As soon as the full moon rose, that power would belong to him.

Torian!

Her raw fear grabbed his attention. He sent his energy to surround his mate, to soothe her. *You're safe. Relax.* Just a few more moments…

I want you to stop.

Her power swirled around him. He reached for the door in her mind.

Stop! It was a scream. Her scream.

Then the door flew open and white hot, pulsing energy shot through him, knocking him straight out of her mind.

* * * *

When Sara felt Torian slump against her, she whirled around in alarm. His body slipped down, and even though she tried to grab him, he hit the floor with a thud.

Oh, God. What had happened? One moment, she'd felt him, and it had been as he were holding her on the inside, just as his arms cradled her body on the outside.

But she'd been afraid. Something weird had been happening inside of her. And she'd started to feel...different. Like her body wasn't her own.

She'd screamed for him to stop, both with her mind and her voice. And now he was lying on the floor, his normally golden skin an ashen color.

"Torian!" She crouched beside him, fear filling her. Had she done this to him? She touched his face. He felt cold, clammy. "Torian, can you hear me?"

He didn't move.

Her fingers searched for his pulse. It was there. Weak. Thready. But there. Good. That meant she hadn't killed him.

Yet.

His lashes lay against his cheeks. His lips were parted, and he barely seemed to breathe.

Oh, God. What had she done? She'd just wanted him to stop, because she'd been so afraid of what was happening. She'd sensed a change coming. And she hadn't wanted to change. She'd just wanted to keep being plain Sara Myers. She hadn't wanted to hurt him.

She tried tapping him lightly on the face. She leaned forward, placing her knees on either side of his body so she could get closer to him. "Torian?" Another tap. Harder this time. "Hello?"

Nothing. Damn. What had she done to him? And what if he didn't wake up? What the hell would she do then?

Her hands wrapped around his head and she cradled him, her fingers sinking into his thick mane of hair. Then a sudden idea slipped into her mind. He'd been communicating with her, right before he blacked out. He'd been in her mind. She'd felt him.

If he could slide so effortlessly into her thoughts, couldn't she do the same, for him? He'd said she had the power of a High Witch. Even if she wasn't exactly sure how to use that power...

She bit her lip. But what other choice did she have? The man was out cold.

"Ready or not," she muttered, taking a quick breath for courage, "here I come." Her fingers tightened around him and she closed her eyes.

And she searched for his mind. Searched for his thoughts. For him.

Torian? There was blackness all around her. A darkness so complete that she felt smothered, enveloped.

Torian? Are you here? She couldn't feel anything anymore. Not the carpet under her knees, not the hard feel of his body beneath her. She seemed to be floating, just drifting through the darkness.

She'd never liked the dark. As a child, she'd always slept with a nightlight. *Monsters lived in the dark.* She really, really wished she had a night light right then. Something, anything, to guide her through this darkness.

And then she heard a scream. A child's scream. High, frightened.

What the hell? Her mind shot forward, following the sound. Light exploded around her and a dozen images rolled through her mind's eye.

She saw a small boy, with dark hair and silver eyes. His face was covered in bruises, and his body was a bloody mass of cuts and gashes. He was sobbing, the sound wrenching at her heart. And a tall man dressed in a black robe, stood over him, laughing.

You'll never have the power, child! Never. I'll kill you just like I killed—

The light vanished, and the choking darkness returned. *No!* The boy's pain was a living, breathing entity within her. She wanted to get back to him, to protect him. He needed her, she could feel it. She had to get back to him.

Light exploded, its brightness almost blinding her. She strained, hoping to see the boy again. Hoping to help him—

A small figure huddled on the ground. Blood soaked the earth surrounding him. Long, dirty black hair hung from the boy's head. His clothes were all but torn from him. He was holding a locket, rubbing it with fingers stained red. She reached out to him, wanting to hold him.

The black-robed man appeared again, laughing. He snatched the locket from the child. *Fool. You mourn for her? She was nothing, nothing! A vessel, just like they all are. We feed on them, on their power.* He smiled, and it was an awful sight. Because his smile was so angelic. So pure. *You'll learn. You'll learn what it's like to hunger for death. To hunger for blood.*

The light vanished.

Darkness. So much darkness. She was blind. She was lost. Lost in the night.

Why was there so much darkness in Torian's mind? So much pain? The darkness and echoes of pain were crushing her.

Torian!

Light flashed again, and she saw Torian racing toward her. His face was tight with rage. His silver eyes flashing with fury.

You shouldn't be here! He grabbed her arm, and a sudden force of power sent her hurtling from his mind.

Her eyes snapped open. She glanced down. Torian's eyes were open and burning with fury.

Her breath caught. She was straddling his body, her legs on either side of his hips. Her hands were still buried in his thick hair. Her face was inches from him, her lips close enough to kiss his.

He was fully conscious now. Fully aware. And, apparently, fully enraged.

But at least he was back with her.

"Torian, I—"

His hands locked around her, and he pulled her down those few more precious inches. Then his mouth was on hers. Hot. Hard. Hungry.

He kissed her as if he had every right. His lips pushed against hers, forcing them apart. His tongue swept inside, rubbing, tasting. Demanding a response.

A low moan rumbled in the back of her throat. She felt her breasts tighten, swell. And she could feel him, lengthening, thickening against the cradle of her body. Like a cat, she rubbed against him, needing to touch him.

Her clothes were too hot. She wanted them off. She wanted to feel him, flesh against flesh.

She just wanted him.

Naked.

Oh, God, the man could kiss. His tongue was thrusting into her mouth now, mimicking the slight movement of his hips against hers. His fingers slipped down her body. His hands cupped her breasts, and he began to tease her, to stroke her through the fabric of her shirt.

She was incredibly glad she wasn't wearing a bra. She just wished that her shirt wasn't in the way.

She'd never felt this way before. Never wanted a man this much. Her body was tight, yearning. And more than anything else in that moment, she wanted to take him deep, deep inside of her. She wanted to feel him moving, thrusting into her sex. And she wanted to come around his thick, hard length.

Her body was readying for him. She could feel her sex moisten, feel her muscles clench.

Torian tore his mouth from hers and buried his face in the curve of her neck. "You smell so good," he muttered, his voice little more than a dark growl. "So damn good." He licked her, his tongue teasing the delicate skin of her throat, and all the while, his fingers rasped against her nipples.

A moan slipped past her lips. She couldn't bite back the sound. She needed him too much. Her hands grabbed his shirt and she jerked it over his head, tossing it onto the floor beside them. Her fingers stroked the muscled expanse of his chest. Traced his small, dark nipples. She realized that she loved to touch him. To caress him.

His body flexed beneath her. His arousal pressed against her sex through her jeans. Damn, but he felt good. Strong.

What would his thick shaft feel like inside of her? She couldn't wait to find out.

Her body was on fire. "Torian—"

He rolled in a lightning fast move. She blinked, finding herself on the floor. He loomed over her, and his hard face was etched with need. No trace of his anger, his rage, remained. There was only hunger. For her.

He grabbed the hem of her shirt and he yanked it up and over her head. His bright gaze locked on her body.

Her breasts were tight, aching. Her nipples pointed toward him as if begging for his attention. And, God, she wanted his mouth on her. Wanted his warm, wet tongue to taste her nipples.

"Torian…lick me." His legs were between hers, spreading her legs wide, and she bucked against him, a feverish desire sweeping over her.

His jaw clenched at her sensual order. Then his dark head slowly lowered. Sara closed her eyes, feeling out of control. Hungry.

Oh, yes, please—

She felt the rasp of his tongue against her nipple. A broken moan rumbled in her throat. Then his lips closed over her breast and he sucked.

Jesus. Her back arched off the carpet, and her fingers dug into his back. This was what she wanted, what she needed.

He licked, he sucked. His tongue swirled around her areola and his lips feverishly tightened on her flesh. He showed her no mercy. But then, she didn't want him to. Because the things he was doing...she felt as if she'd climax any second.

Just with his mouth on her.

Her hips lifted, pushed against him, and his hand moved, stroking her other breast while he continued to suck her nipple. To tease her, to torment her.

And she loved every second of it.

She heard herself moaning, panting. When she'd made love with Tom, she'd barely felt any pleasure. And she'd sure as hell never nearly climaxed just from the touch of his mouth on her breasts.

She opened her eyes, wanting to see Torian. Her lover.

His dark head lifted, and his hair brushed against her nipple. "You taste so good." His silver eyes burned with lust. "I can't get enough of you." His hand slid down the curve of her stomach and he stroked her belly button, his fingers touching the small golden hoop. Then he lowered his head and his tongue swirled against the ring.

Oh, God. Tension was building in her. Mounting. She needed him, wanted him deep inside of her. *Now.*

She felt him unsnap her jeans and heard the faint rasp of her zipper.

"I shouldn't do this," he growled. "Not yet."

Yes, yes, he should. She was burning up. Her body was shaking. Desperate need was making her ache.

"I want you to," she whispered, and it was the truth. She wanted him to make love to her in that moment more than she'd ever wanted anything else. Her body was desperate for release. Desperate for him. *Torian.*

He shoved down her jeans and she kicked them out of the way. She felt the fabric of his pants against her thighs, strangely soft, strangely smooth, fabric.

His arms braced on either side of her head. The bulge of his arousal pressed against her. All that separated them was the thin lace of her panties and his pants. She wanted them both gone. She wanted all of him against her. In her.

"Torian!" The cry that slipped past her lips was a frantic demand. She couldn't take much more. Her body was going crazy with need.

Her hands slid across his chest. Muscles rippled, flexed. A dark coating of hair covered that delicious expanse.

She lifted her head and found his nipple with her tongue. She stroked him, teased him, just as he'd done to her. And she was rewarded by the stiffening of his body, by the harsh growl of hunger that rumbled from his throat. Her fingers edged down the flat plane of his stomach. Her tongue licked his nipple. She wanted to touch him, all of him.

His hands snapped up, clenched around her wrists, and his gaze met hers, so silver there wasn't even a trace of his black pupils. His nostrils flared. His cheeks were flushed, and stark hunger was stamped on his face.

A thrill of power shot through her. She'd never had a man look at her like that before. Not with that blind hunger, that desperate need.

He pushed her wrists down onto the soft carpet. His muscled thighs spread her legs out another inch, two, opening her fully to him.

And then he kissed her. A hot, open-mouthed kiss that she met with full force. She felt his hips thrust against her. God, she wanted him inside her, thrusting that long, thick—

He tore his mouth away, breathing heavily. "It's too soon." She arched beneath him, and he groaned. "It's not the right time."

Oh, yes, it was most definitely the right time. Nothing had ever been more "right" in her whole life.

"Torian, I need you." It was a plea. He couldn't leave her now, not with this hunger, this desire coursing through her blood. "Make love to me."

His jaw clenched. Blue sparks flashed around them like fireworks and his body shuddered. Then he released her wrists, grasped her panties and jerked, shredding the thin fabric in one quick movement.

This was it, she realized, heart pounding so loudly that it sounded like a drum in her ears. He was going to make love to her now. He was going to end this desperate need.

His hands pressed against her sensitive inner thighs. Then he stared down at her exposed flesh, licking his lips as if he could already taste her.

His strong fingers parted her feminine folds, and he stroked her lightly, spreading the creamy moisture across her hungry sex. Then he inserted one large finger into her body. She closed her eyes, shuddering.

"You're so tight," he whispered, his gaze still on her sex. "So hot." His tongue snaked across his lips again. *"And you're mine."*

He thrust his finger inside her, and she arched at the touch. She could feel her body throbbing, feel the tension coiling tighter and tighter within her.

But it wasn't enough. She needed more.

A second finger pushed into her. "Come on," he whispered. "Open for me."

It had been so long since she'd been touched by a man. She hadn't been with anyone since Tom, and their marriage had ended over three years ago. She felt a strange pressure when Torian pushed his broad fingers into her. Then her body shifted, quickly accommodating his touch.

But she still needed *more.* Her head thrashed against the carpet.

He laughed softly. "My sweet witch. God, you're beautiful." He eased his fingers away from her body. "And I just have to taste you…"

Then his dark head lowered and she felt the brush of his tongue against her sex, felt him lick her. Suck her—

Her climax broke over in a wave of white hot pleasure. Her entire body shook, pulsed, as the waves of her orgasm rocked through her. She closed her eyes, squeezing the lids shut. *Oh, God. Oh, God.* The feelings running through her body were so intense. She couldn't stop shuddering, couldn't stop moaning.

And all the while, his tongue thrust against her, thrust *into* her.

Fire licked over her body. She burned with a pleasure unlike anything she'd ever imagined, and her climax seemed to last forever, pouring through her, overwhelming her. The muscles of her body tightened, clenched.

"Torian!" Her eyes snapped open. Bright blue light flashed around her, and she shuddered one last time.

The climax left her weak, limp. And feeling damn good.

Torian rose above her. She found that she couldn't look away from his hungry stare.

"Wow." It was the only thing she could think to say. She'd never had an orgasm like that, never felt so much pleasure with a man. And she realized that she couldn't wait to feel that way again, with him.

His lips curved.

And then she flushed, realizing that he was still aroused. "Torian, you didn't..."

He shook his head. His body was tense, the muscles locked in iron control. "I can't, not yet."

She reached for him. He'd given her so much pleasure. She didn't want to leave him in need. "Let me..."

Again, he shook his head. Then he stroked her cheek. "I can't have you yet, witch. The time isn't right." A muscle flexed along his jaw. "But soon I'm going to thrust deep into that tight body of yours, and I'll have my pleasure."

Heat zipped through her at his sensual promise. Sara stared at his face, gazing at the hard planes and angles, gazing at his strong chin. His brilliant eyes. And her body pulsed.

She swallowed. "You know, I must say, that was...pretty amazing." If that was what it was like to make love with a wizard, then she was surprised more women weren't literally attacking Torian and his kind. She still tingled in spots.

"Yes." His gaze dropped to her breasts. She saw hunger flare in his eyes. "It was." He inhaled sharply. "Do you have any idea how good you smell...and taste?"

Oh, boy. Her heart leapt. "I-I'd never done...that before." Her husband had been more of the slam-bam type.

"I'm the first to taste you?" he asked, his eyes widening.

Damn. Why did every thing he said turn her on? She nodded.

His lips split into a satisfied smile. "Good."

Her gaze dropped to his waist and the unmistakable bulge pressing against the front of his pants. "I-I could do the...same...for you."

He shuddered, and she realized that she really wanted to taste him. Wanted to feel his thick length. Wanted to caress him with her mouth.

He pulled back, rising quickly to his feet.

"Torian?"

"I can't. My control—" He took a deep breath, then shook his head. "It won't last."

She didn't care. She wanted him out of control. As out of control as she'd been. Jumping up, she faced him, uncaring of her nudity. "It doesn't matter."

He stepped away from her. "Yes," he said very definitely. "It does."

"Torian…" She wanted to touch him. But when she lifted her hand, he moved back. Pain shot through her at his rejection.

"I can't," he repeated, his voice gruff. "You don't understand."

No, she didn't understand. The man, correction, *wizard*, who'd just given her the best climax of her life wouldn't let her touch him. "Make me understand," she ordered, her temper beginning to stir.

His hands clenched. "I'll hurt you."

Sara's brow furrowed. "Don't be ridiculous—"

"You don't know what I'm like, what I'm really like." His molten gaze drifted over her naked body, and she felt that hot stare like a physical touch. "If we don't wait for the Becoming, I won't be able to keep my control. If that happens…" He shook his head. "It's not a chance I'm willing to take."

There was that damn Becoming again. She was really getting tired of hearing about that. "Forget the Becoming! Can't we just be a man and a woman? Can't we just be together?"

"No," he said softly. "We can't." Then he paced toward the door. "Not until it's safe."

Not until it's safe. "What do you mean…safe?"

He glanced back at her, and his lips thinned.

A cold knot formed in the pit of her stomach. "Torian? Tell me what you mean."

But his mouth stayed stubbornly closed, his strong jaw clenched.

She wanted to scream at him. Wanted to throw something. He wasn't answering her. And he wasn't going to make love to her. "Why?" The cry was ripped from her. "Why did you touch me if you weren't going to make love to me?"

"I needed to taste you." He turned fully toward her. "And I could feel your hunger." His shoulders lifted and fell in a small shrug. "As your mate, I couldn't let you hunger, couldn't let you need."

But he could be left hungering, needing. Her teeth clenched. "It's not fair." She didn't want to leave him aching. She wanted to give him the pleasure that he'd given her. *I want to make you feel the way I felt.*

He stopped, his hand on the doorknob. "You will," he said, glancing back over his shoulder, and she knew that he'd picked up on her thoughts. Again. "You'll give me everything I need…during the Becoming."

He opened the door and walked outside.

"Dammit!" She turned and grabbed her clothes. The man was an idiot. A complete moron. He'd given her the best orgasm of her life, and then he'd walked away. Because it wasn't time yet. Because it wasn't the *Becoming*.

Screw the Becoming. She still didn't really even know what the damn thing was.

Sara pulled on her shirt and reached for her panties. They were shredded beyond repair. "You are so going to have to replace these," she muttered. She'd spent twenty dollars on them at Victoria's Secret, and she'd only worn them once.

She jerked on her jeans and stepped into her shoes. Part of her knew that Torian had left because he'd needed to cool off. She'd seen his arousal, seen the need still etched onto his face.

Yes, part of her knew that he'd left to regain more of that precious control of his, but she didn't care. She was stewing for a fight. And since he'd dragged her away from her home and into the middle of nowhere, he was the only one she could fight with.

She whirled on her heel and marched toward the door. Then a thought hit her and she froze.

Slowly, she turned back around, staring at the chunk of wood in the fireplace.

Torian had been in her mind earlier, and she'd felt something…something stirring inside of her.

But then the sexual hunger had swept through her and she'd forgotten all about the magic. She'd thought only of Torian, of what he was doing to her.

But what if…

Her hands trembled as she took a tentative step toward the stone fireplace. Could she do it now? Could she really control fire? Torian had. She'd watched through her front window as he used fire to fight the Dark Ones. He'd just seemed to wave his arms and the flames appeared.

Could she do that? Did she really have that power? She took another step toward the log. He'd said the first step for her would be mastering fire. That meant it had to be easy, right? Weren't all first steps easy?

Sara waved her hand toward the fire, using the sweeping gesture that she'd seen Torian make in her front yard. Nothing happened.

She did it again, sweeping her hands out in a large circle.

Nothing.

Well, damn. Her hands dropped to her sides.

Apparently, she wasn't any more magical than she'd been before Torian had gone tiptoeing through her mind. So much for his awakening her power. If she even had any power to awaken.

She turned away from the fireplace. She'd better go find him and tell him that whatever he'd done hadn't worked. Maybe he really did have the wrong woman. Maybe she wasn't a witch after all.

Sighing softly, she glanced back at the fireplace. The wood sat, cold and hard, on the grate.

Frustrated anger swept through her. Why wouldn't the damn thing burn? It was a log. Logs were supposed to burn. Fire should burn. It should burn bright and hard and fierce.

It should burn.

A tendril of smoke rose from the log. Her eyes widened. What was—

A loud crack sounded from the fireplace, and the wood was suddenly enveloped in a bright ball of orange flame.

Oh, my God. Sara stared at the fire, stunned. She'd done that, she'd made the fire. Actually made the log burn. Her gaze was trained on the small fire, and amazement, awe, filled her.

Burn, she thought, her excitement building as the flames fed hungrily on the wood. *Burn!*

The flames flared higher. Brighter. A full smile curved her lips. She'd done it! Made fire! Made the cold log burn, and she couldn't wait to tell Torian,

She really was a witch, just like her mother. She had power, magic—

The flames shot out of the fireplace and raced across the carpet.

Sara stopped smiling.

Bright orange flames leapt around the room, burning wood, furniture. She could smell the fire, smell it all around her. She felt the heat from the flames against her skin and terror rolled through her.

Down, she thought, prayed. *Go down.* But the flames just rose, eating hungrily at the room.

She stumbled back, heading for the door. The cabin was burning in front of her. She had to get out!

But the flames circled her, trapping her within the room.

All of the walls were burning now, and the flames were flaring even brighter than before.

Numbing terror filled her as she realized that she couldn't get out. Could. Not. Get. Out. If she ran for the door, she'd be burned. Sara coughed, inhaling the cloying smoke that filled the cabin. The crackle of flames filled her ears, and the sound echoed eerily like a man's laughter.

Oh, God. She stared at the flames. There was nowhere for her to run. If she moved, they would burn her. She coughed again, choking on the thick smoke.

There was nowhere to go.

She'd started the fire, but she couldn't stop it. The cabin was burning around her, and the flames were inching ever closer to her body.

"Torian!" She tried to scream his name, but her voice emerged as a hoarse whisper. *Torian!* This time, the scream was in her mind, and she prayed that he would hear her, that he would feel her and come back in time to help her. Dammit, he was a freaking wizard. He'd been hopping in and out of her mind since they'd met. And he told her that she "broadcasted" her thoughts. Well, she was sure as hell broadcasting now. *Help me, Torian!*

She fell to her knees, her chest heaving. She couldn't breathe. Her skin was hot, burning. The flames were so bright. Orange. Red. Beautiful and bright.

She closed her eyes and struggled for breath. *Torian, please, help me.* Her mental cry was weaker. *She* was weaker.

And then Sara heard a man's voice clearly above the growing roar the flames.

"You're going to burn, witch. Die in the fire, like all of your kind."

Oh, God, no!

"Witches burn..." His taunting voice was the last sound she heard.

Six

He'd come too close to taking her. Far, far too close, Torian realized.

He shouldn't have touched her again. Shouldn't have kissed her. But he hadn't been able to help himself. When he'd first sensed her in his mind, he'd been terrified. Terrified that she would learn the truth about him, about his past. And he'd been afraid that when she learned that truth, she would turn from him, that she would try to leave him.

Sara couldn't be allowed to leave him. He needed her too much.

When he'd opened his eyes and found her crouched above him, his first instinct had been to claim her, to chain her to him so that she couldn't leave, couldn't flee.

Rage had ridden him hard. He'd been furious with himself, with his weakness. Her power had caught him unprepared and it had, quite literally, knocked him on his ass. He'd tried to reclaim any ground that he may have lost. He didn't know how long she'd been in his mind, didn't know what secrets she'd seen.

He'd wanted to remind her of their physical bond. Of the passion that they would share. Hell, he'd just wanted her.

So he'd given in to his desire, to the hungry need that filled him every time she was near. And he'd kissed her. Touched her. Licked her sweet nipples. Spread her thighs and tasted her cream.

Torian closed his eyes. Okay, remembering Sara's beautiful body was definitely not the way to cool down. Hell, he'd left the cabin so that he could get his body back under control. Not so he could relive the heated moments he'd spent in her arms.

Damn, he'd screwed up royally with her. He knew it. And, of course, he'd compounded things by walking away from her. But if he'd stayed with her for even a moment more, he wasn't certain he could have stopped himself from taking her.

Sara. His sweet witch. How was he going to be able to resist her for the next few days?

And what would she do when she finally learned the truth? Would she stay with him? Would she leave him?

He clenched his hands, stopped his frantic pacing and stood beside a thin pine tree. Birds were chirping above him, and squirrels were scurrying up a nearby oak.

The mountains here were beautiful. He'd hoped to share that raw beauty with Sara. Maybe he still could. Maybe he could go back to her, get her to go with him on a hike.

They could try to start over.

And he could try, try very hard, not to throw her down on the nearest bed.

Of course, she might not speak to him when he returned to the cabin. He'd seen the anger in her eyes when he left. The anger and the pain.

Slowly, very slowly, he unclenched his fists. He hadn't meant to hurt her. She was—

A shrill cry split the air. A dozen birds flew overhead, their movements frantic, frightened.

Every muscle in his body tensed. Then he caught a faint scent on the wind. Fear shot through him. He knew that scent.

Fire.

There was a fire somewhere, and it was close. Too close.

Sara. He sent his mind searching for her. She didn't like it when he slipped into her thoughts, but this was an emergency. He needed to make certain that she was all right, that she was safe.

His mind journeyed across the distance, searched for her and found...

Flames. A smoke-filled room. Terror. And evil. Waiting in the darkness. Waiting for his mate's death.

"No!" Torian wasn't aware that he'd screamed. Fear was a living, breathing being inside him. He could feel Sara's life force slipping away as the flames flared brighter around her.

No, he wasn't going to lose her. He wouldn't lose her. He'd just found her.

In an instant, he flashed back the cabin. *I'm coming, Sara. I'm coming. Hold on. Just hold on.*

He saw the smoke first, billowing up like an angry fist. The stench of the fire filled his nostrils and the heat of the flames seemed to lance his skin as he shoved open the door of the cabin, sending the old wood splintering.

Torian couldn't touch Sara's mind. When he searched for her, he found only darkness, not the usual light that was so much a part of her.

Flames snapped at him, but with a wave of his hand, he pushed them back, struggling with his magic to control the blaze.

His eyes watered and his throat burned. The fire had spread throughout the main room. The heat was intense, consuming. And he couldn't see his mate.

"Sara!" he screamed, cursing the flames, the smoke. Where was she? Was she still alive?

Dammit, she had to be alive! "Sara!" He rushed forward, still battling the flames with his power. He didn't know how long he'd be able to hold back the fire.

"Torian..." A bare whisper. From the heart of the flames.

His heart seemed to stop. But had he really heard her voice, or had it just been his imagination? He stepped forward, crouching low as the smoke began to choke him. "Sara? Can you hear me?"

"Torian..."

It *was* her voice. He used the power of the wind to push back the flames as he crawled toward her, trying to stay as close to the floor as possible. He found her, crumpled next to the sofa. Her eyes were closed, her beautiful features stained with soot.

"*Sara.*" Relief filled him. He'd found her. She was still alive. "I'm here, Sara." And he was going to get her out of this damn cabin and away from the flames.

He pulled her into his arms, cradling her precious weight. If he hadn't found her....

She coughed, her body jerking. Damn. She was almost wheezing. Torian knew she'd inhaled too much smoke. Hell, he'd only been in the cabin a few minutes and he could barely breathe. It had to be ten times worse for her.

The fire began to flare, the flames shooting higher as they fought against his wind spell. He knew he didn't have much time. The fire was too strong. It wouldn't stay banked for long.

He fought his way back to the cabin's entrance. The broken door swayed drunkenly on its hinges. He shouldered it out of the way, his arms tightening around Sara.

Once they were clear of the cabin, he ran as fast as he could. Behind him, he heard the sound of breaking glass. Heard the crackle of the flames, and he knew that the fire would soon rage out of control.

When he was certain he'd traveled a safe distance, he put his precious burden down on the soft grass and crouched beside her, stroking her face. Soot covered her. Her clothes were singed. Dark circles hung beneath her eyes, and her lips were white.

She'd almost died.

A violent coughing fit swept over her, and she jerked in his arms.

He knew he needed to clear the smoke from her lungs, and he held his hands above her body. A small, white ball of light appeared.

Sara's eyes flashed open, bright with terror. "T-Torian!" Her voice was raspy, broken.

"Shhh. It's all right, I've got you." And he'd never let her go.

But he could tell by the glazed expression in her blue eyes that she didn't really see him. She was trapped in a nightmare, probably still seeing the flames and feeling the brush of fire against her skin.

"N-no." She shook her head frantically. "I d-don't w-want to die!"

Pain closed his own throat and he could only stare down at her as a hot rage simmered in his heart.

"Please, don't l-let me b-burn!" She whispered.

The white ball slid over her body, healing her burns and removing the smoke from her lungs.

"It's all right, Sara," he said softly. "You're safe now." Torian waved his hand and the ball disappeared.

She turned her head and her gaze, soft with unshed tears, met his. "He said…he said…I'd burn." Her voice was stronger, clearer, but heavy with remembered terror.

He stiffened. "Sara…no one was in the cabin. The flames were everywhere—"

A tear slid down her cheek. "He was laughing. He said witches burn. That I would burn." She grasped his arm tightly. "Don't…let me burn."

Her pain, her fear, pierced him. "I won't." He stroked her cheek and felt the wet warmth of her tear on his finger.

"Promise me," she said, obviously fighting to say the words. Her lids were lowering, her voice slurring. "Promise you…won't let…"

"Shhh." He wanted her to sleep. To heal. "You're safe. I promise I won't let anything happen to you." He would protect her with his life.

She nodded. Her eyes closed and her hand dropped away from his arm.

He stared down at her still form and her words echoed

through his mind. *He said...he said...I'd burn. He said witches burn.*

Torian looked back at the cabin, back at the flames.

And he remembered his past. Remembered his father's voice, so cruel, so cold. *Have you ever seen a witch burn, boy? It's the best way to kill them. They scream when the flames get them, when their power drains away. Witches burn, boy. They burn...fast and easy. The fire's the best way to kill them. Remember that.*

A chill slid over him. Sara had said a man was in the cabin, that she'd heard his voice. Could it be possible that his bastard father had—

No. No, it couldn't be. His father was dead. He couldn't hurt anyone else. Torian had made sure of that.

The flames flared even higher.

He said witches burn.

There was no way it could've been Lazern. He was dead. Had been dead for ten years.

She'd probably just imagined the voice. She'd been afraid. Delirious.

The flames crackled, licking hungrily toward the sky.

Torian placed a soft kiss on Sara's lips and rose slowly to his feet. Chanting softly, he called forth the wind and the water. The fire was far too powerful for a simple disbursement spell. But he could try using the other elements on it. He had to try something. The fire was too large. If he let the fire keep burning, it would destroy the forest, the animals, everything in its path.

Dark clouds rolled across the blue sky. Thunder rumbled in the distance.

Torian lifted his hands, feeling raw power pour through him. Then the skies opened and powerful sheets of rain pelted down upon the cabin, upon the entire mountain.

He felt the beads of moisture sliding down his face, washing away the soot and the ash. He saw the flames flicker beneath the onslaught. Saw the fire shimmer. He raised his hands, pulling forth the storm's strength.

The rain plummeted down. The fire was no match for its fierce strength, and in moments, it was reduced to embers. Smoke drifted sullenly in the air, wrapping around the cabin's wreckage.

Convinced now that the fire would do no more damage, he turned back to Sara. He'd carefully shielded her from the storm so that she stayed dry and safe on the soft ground behind him.

He picked her up and cradled her against his chest. Exhaustion beat at him. He'd used too much power. His body was slowing, readying for the rejuvenation of deep sleep.

But he couldn't sleep, not yet. He needed to get her cleaned up. Needed to find a safe place for her to rest.

And the safest place he knew of…was Taren.

But did he have enough strength to get them there?

And if he did, would Sara forgive him for taking her to his world?

Damn. He knew she wasn't ready to go to Taren, knew she was still trying to cling to her old life, her old ways.

But when he thought of what could have happened, what had *almost* happened, raw fear licked through him. He would have to do a much better job of protecting his mate.

Witches burn.

Yes, he had to protect her, even if his form of protection enraged her.

* * * *

For the second time, Sara awoke to find herself in bed with Torian. But this time, she didn't scream. Instead, she snuggled back beneath the covers and reached for him. She stroked his arm, liking the feel of his warm skin beneath her fingers. She stretched slowly against him, yawning.

Then she glanced at his face and found his unblinking silver stare on her.

"H-hello," she whispered. Her throat felt strange. Not painful, but tight, like she hadn't used her voice in a while. The silk sheets rubbed against her body. Her completely naked body.

Uh, oh.

"Hello, yourself." He paused. "How do you feel?"

She frowned, wondering why he'd asked. "All right. And you?"

His gaze narrowed. "Do you remember what happened yesterday?"

Yesterday? Her lips pursed as she tried to recall. Yesterday, they'd almost made love. He'd given her a shuddering climax. She frowned, remembering. Then they'd fought. And she'd been so angry.

She'd seen the fireplace. And—

"Oh. My. God." Her eyes widened as horror filled her. She shot straight up in bed, holding the sheet to her chest. "I burned down your cabin!"

She remembered the paintings that had been on the walls. The wood carvings that had sat on the table. All of the furniture. "I burned it all," she whispered, dropping her gaze. She couldn't look at him, not after what she'd done. The man probably hated her.

His fingers cupped her chin, forcing her to meet his stare. "Tell me what happened."

There was no anger in his tone, just curiosity. She bit her lip, feeling absolutely horrible. She'd burned down the man's house, for goodness sake! So much for being an all powerful witch.

"I just wanted to…to see if I could do it. Um, start the fire, that is." She swallowed. "I stared at the wood, thinking about the fire and how much I wanted it to burn." Heat rose in her cheeks. "And I did those, you know, hand gestures that you like to do."

One black brow quirked, but he didn't speak.

She inhaled sharply. "The next thing I knew, the whole damn room was on fire." The flames had spread so fast, and it had seemed as if there would be no escape from that inferno.

"I tried to stop it," she whispered. "I tried to use my p-power, but I couldn't do it." She sighed. "I just couldn't get rid of the flames. When I tried, they just seemed to burn brighter."

He frowned, his hand dropping away from her chin. "How long did it take the fire to spread?"

"Not long, maybe a few seconds." The flames had flashed around the room so quickly, greedily destroying everything in sight.

She felt terrible. Torian probably hated her now. She just wanted to slink away, to go hide and pretend that this whole mess had never started. She'd known she couldn't do this. She was not made to be some kind of all-powerful witch. After all, her first spell had almost killed her. If it hadn't been for Torian…

"Did you hear anything, anything at all, when the flames started to spread?"

She glanced up, her attention caught by the tension in his voice. He was staring at her, his lips compressed into a thin line, his face a hard mask.

"What is it?" Something was wrong. Very wrong.

"Did you hear anything?" He repeated, his voice curt. "Just tell me."

She remembered the flames. The smoke. It had choked her, sent her stumbling to her knees. Her eyes had burned. She'd nearly been blinded by the thick, dark smoke. And there had been—

Laughter.

Sara shook her head. No, that couldn't be right.

You're going to burn, witch.

"I-I thought I heard a voice. A man's voice." But that couldn't have been possible. She'd been alone in the cabin when Torian left. She'd probably just imagined the voice.

He swore softly, closing his eyes, and she got a really, really bad feeling in the pit of her stomach. "Uh, look, Torian, I'm sorry about the cabin. The fire just got out of control."

His eyes snapped open. "The fire wasn't your fault."

"I started it," she reminded him. Of course, the blaze had been her fault!

He nodded. "Yeah, but someone else fed the flames and pushed them out of control."

Okay. That bad feeling was getting worse. "S-someone else?" *Witches burn.*

His face was grim.

"And j-just who might this someone else have been?" Not another Dark One. Not another—

Shadows seemed to move in the depths of his eyes. But he didn't answer her.

Hell. "Torian? Was it a-another Dark One?" But the guy in the cabin hadn't been doing that weird screaming thing. And she'd gotten such a strong sense of...evil.

"I don't think it was just *any* Dark One. "

She didn't like the sound of this.

"The way the fire was blazing," he continued, his voice hard, "it had to be someone who was very, very powerful."

Well, that was just great. "How powerful are we talking here?"

Torian opened his mouth to speak, then hesitated.

She frowned. "Torian?"

He climbed from the bed, jerking on a pair of pants as he rose.

He paced across the small room, tension evident in the hard lines of his body. "Sara, not all wizards are good."

"But, I thought wizards...were the good guys." After all, Torian was a good guy. He'd saved her life, pulled her out of that God-awful fire.

He stopped pacing. Turned to face her. "It's a little more complicated than that."

Wasn't it always? "Just tell me what's happening," she said. She had a right to know. After all, they were talking about her life.

"A wizard is born with power, great power." His lips thinned. "But some wizards are always hungry for more strength."

Uh, oh. She really didn't think she was going to like this story. "And just how do wizards get more strength?"

"Sometimes they make a trade with darkness."

"Darkness? Is that like...evil?"

"In a sense. The universe is full of power. Light and dark power. Wizards and witches are born with the power of light. But sometimes that power isn't enough. Sometimes wizards decide they want more strength. So they use the dark powers. The dark gifts. And they often even...steal power."

Her eyes narrowed. "You told me before that Dark Ones steal power from witches." A shiver slid over her. "These Dark Ones, what are they, really?"

"They were once wizards."

Not good. "Wizards. Like you?"

He nodded.

Damn. So much for the good guys. "So guys like you just decide they want to be stronger and go out and kill a few witches and steal their power? And they turn 'dark,' or something like that?"

"They're not like me." His voice was hard. His face was tight with tension. "I'd never hurt you. Never steal—"

"My power?" She finished for him. "Right, and do you mind telling me just how these guys steal power? I mean, what do they do? Jump into my head and—"

"No."

Sara blinked at him. "No, you're not gonna tell me or no, they don't jump into my head?"

A hard sigh. "You don't want to know how the Dark Ones steal power."

"Yeah, I do." Her jaw clenched. "I deserve to know." Those guys were targeting her, she needed to know exactly what they wanted to do if they ever got their hands on her.

Torian stalked toward the bed and stared down at her. "A

Dark One touches a witch's heart, touches her with the spell of life. That touch, that spell, pierces her very soul, and her magic starts to bleed out of her...and into the wizard."

She swallowed.

"But in order to take all of a witch's magic, to get every last drop," his silver stare pinned her to the bed, "you have to kill the witch. And the best way to kill a witch...is with fire."

Her hands were shaking. *Her whole body was shaking.* "B- but at the c-cabin, h-he didn't try to touch—"

"Your power is barely awakened. That Dark One was trying to kill you, not drain you." His eyes narrowed. "And I think he attacked you because he knows what I've got planned."

What I've got planned. And just what did he have planned?

"Dark Ones, they don't have true mates. Because they can't get the power of the Becoming, they steal witches from their true mates, and they—"

"Hold on!" Her head was starting to ache. "Back up to that bit about wizards getting the power of the Becoming." A cold lump had formed in her chest at his words. "Why don't you just explain that one to me, nice and slow." Cause she had a sudden feeling that she might know *exactly* what Torian had planned.

His lips thinned. "It's not what you think."

"I hope not." Because it very much sounded like Torian was planning to use her and then take her power at the Becoming.

"The Becoming is an exchange. I give you my power, my strength, and you give me yours. It's physical. Mental. It's you, Becoming me. It's me, Becoming you. We're both stronger after it, our powers are enhanced." He sat on the bed. "We're joined. We become one entity, and our powers are one, too."

That sounded...very intense. Maybe too intense. "And just how...does this Becoming happen?" She knew it had something to do with sex. Otherwise Torian would have made love to her yesterday.

He gazed into her eyes. "We'll make love. Under the full moon. First you'll dance for me, your body naked in the moon's light. Then I'll come to you. Claim you. The moon will shine on us and we'll bond." He stroked her cheek. "I've heard...that...there may be pain."

She'd been with him, imagining for a moment what it would be like to make love with him under the glowing light of the full moon. To feel his hands on her body. To feel him, deep inside. Yep, she'd been with him, right until the moment he'd mentioned pain. "Why is there pain?" Call her crazy, but she just wasn't a big pain fan.

"The powers. Sometimes they can be overwhelming." His hand lifted and his fingers pressed lightly against her temple. "Your powers, they're particularly strong. When they are fully unleashed…" His hand dropped. "I'm not really sure what will happen."

She *really* didn't like the sound of that. "So let me get this straight. I dance naked in the moonlight, and then my powers go wild and send me spiraling into some kind of hell?" That was so not her idea of a good time. "Whatever happened to candlelight and soft music?"

"I'll be with you," he said, the words gruff. "We'll be together. We'll share everything."

"But what if the guy who attacked me gets to me first?"

"He won't." He sounded determined. Hard.

"But what if he does?" She licked her lips. "Will he kill me?"

"He's not going to get to you."

She didn't know what she feared more. The Dark Ones. Or the Becoming. "Why can't I just be back at home, sitting on my couch and watching television?" Why had her life suddenly become so crazy? So dangerous?

"Because you're special, Sara. Very special."

She didn't feel special. What she felt was damned unlucky. "I thought you said we'd be safe at the cabin." She glared at him.

"We should have been." He rubbed his hand over his face. "But this Dark One…He's different."

"Different? Different how?"

"He's Dark. I can sense it. But he doesn't have the usual weakness, the taint of one who has been transformed into a Dark One."

Great. "So he's like a super Dark One?" Wonderful. She couldn't control fire, but Torian thought she'd be able to survive in a face off against a super strong Dark One. Just how the hell did he expect her to do that?

"Something like that." His jaw flexed. "The Dark Ones have been gathering strength on my world. They've been attacking the Guardians more. I think they're banding together."

Sara shook her head, not liking the sound of this at all. "Wouldn't that mean they'd need some kind of leader?"

He nodded.

"Let me guess," she muttered. "Super Dark is leading them, right?"

"I think so."

Oh, damn.

He grabbed her arms. "You've got to help me, Saralynn. You have to help me fight him, to defeat the Dark Ones before they destroy both our worlds."

"Are you crazy? I can't start a fire right much less fight some army of minions! I will die, Torian. Die! I can't fight them." She'd thought she could, before the Super Dark guy nearly killed her in less than five minutes at the cabin. But now, well—

"You can defeat them once the Becoming is complete."

Yeah, and right now, she was scared of that, too.

"There are others in my world who are on our side. They'll help us. We won't be alone."

"What happens," she asked, shoving a lock of hair behind her ear in one quick move, "if we fight them, and they win?"

He stilled. "You don't want to know."

"Yes, I do." Her hands clenched around the sheet. "Worst case scenario, Fury. The big, bad Dark Ones kick our asses. What happens then?"

"The world will end."

Oh, hell.

"There will be no more light. Only darkness." His gaze was bleak. "In my world, and then in yours, there will be death and darkness."

Okay. That was bad. Very, very bad. She took a deep breath. "I guess we don't really have a choice, do we?"

"I've never had a choice."

She frowned, wondering at the guarded note she'd heard in his voice. "What do you mean you never had a choice?"

A sad smile twisted his lips. "We are what we're born to be."

And, apparently, she'd been born to be a witch. "Your world, is it very different from mine?" she asked.

"In some ways. In others, it's nearly identical."

Okay, that didn't sound so bad. Sara nodded and glanced idly around the room, trying to figure out her next move. If she went with him to his world, there would be no going back. Her life would change forever. Was she really ready for that? And was there any other choice?

She sighed, wrapped the sheet around her body and rose from the bed. The floor was cold beneath her bare feet. She shivered, hugging the sheet tighter to her. The wood creaked as she walked toward the window and the glow of sunlight. Outside, she could just see an endless stretch of mountains. Trees. Blue skies. "So where are we anyway?" she asked, her gaze on the savage beauty of the land. "Another safe cabin?"

He didn't answer.

Sara glanced back over her shoulder. "Torian? Where are we this time?" She tried a smile, wanting to lighten the heavy mood. "You know, since I've met you, I keep waking up to find myself in strange beds."

He didn't smile back. His hands clenched. "I'm sorry, Sara."

"Sorry?" Damn. That bad feeling was back.

"I really didn't have a choice."

Oh, no. She turned around to face him. "What have you done?"

"I had to make certain you were safe."

"*What did you do?*" Please, please don't let him say—

"I brought you home."

"Home?" She jerked her thumb toward the expanse of mountains. "This is *not* my home."

"No." His gaze was unflinching as it met hers. "But it's mine."

She shook her head, denying his words, denying the truth that was wrapping around her. "No, that's not possible. You didn't."

"I brought you across the web. I brought you—"

"No!" Dammit, he hadn't asked her, he'd just—

He stalked toward her.

Her heart was racing frantically, her hands shaking.

Torian stopped before her, lifted his hand and stroked her cheek. His bright silver gaze met hers. "Welcome to my home, Sara. Welcome to my world."

Seven

Torian had expected Sara to cry, to scream. He'd expected her anger, her fear. He hadn't expected the stinging kick that she delivered to his shin.

"You jerk! You damned arrogant jerk!" She pulled back her foot, apparently ready to kick him again.

Torian hurriedly jumped back. "Sara, there was no choice!"

Her beautiful blue eyes narrowed to slits. "Don't give me that crap! You had a choice. You could have left me in *my* world! You could have waited until I was conscious and then talked to me!"

"You were in danger."

"I'm still in danger!" she snapped. "According to you, this whole world you've brought me to is swarming with Dark Ones." She dropped the sheet.

He blinked, staring at her body. "Uh, Sara, is this really the time to—"

"Look at this!" Her hand pointed to the sword shaped birth mark on her abdomen.

He dragged his gaze away from her pink tipped breasts. He could see the curling thatch of blond hair that guarded her sex. He could see…

She snapped her fingers and then poked the birthmark. "This, Torian! Remember this, my wonderful little homing beacon for all that's evil?"

He swallowed and forced his eyes to look at the faint pink mark.

"Now that you've brought me here, how long do you think it'll be before every Dark One in the area feels me?"

He'd thought of that. But she was still safer here with him. His magic was stronger on his own ground. His spells could better protect her. "They already know about you. They can sense you no matter what world you're in." The Becoming was too close now. Hell, he could smell the power on her. And it was drawing him, pulling him in, making him want to take her—

The door to the bedroom flew open. "Hey, Torian, is your mate up yet?" The tall blond man who'd entered the room gaped at them. "Uh, I guess she is." His golden stare locked on Sara's exposed body.

Torian stiffened. "Get out."

He heard Sara swear as she made a quick grab for the sheet.

"Get. Out." He loved Fabian like a brother, but if the man didn't leave the room in the next two seconds, he was going to kill him.

As Torian's anger boiled, blue sparks began to flash in the air around him.

"Damn," Sara muttered, "don't people here know how to knock?"

Fabian's nostrils flared, as if he'd just caught her scent. "She's so close…"

"Fabian…" He sent a surge of magic toward the other man, a surge strong enough to send him stumbling back.

Fabian's arms shot out and he braced himself against the door frame. He shook his head, blinking as if he was confused. "I-I'm sorry." He turned on his heel and marched down the hall.

Torian waved his hand and slammed the door shut. He jerked his head toward Sara. "Never…let another see you…unclothed."

Her lip curled and her pointed little chin lifted. "Oh, right. Because you know, I just love parading around naked in front of strangers. It just gives me a thrill." She'd wrapped her body in the sheet, tucking the edge between her breasts. "And seriously, what is up with the sparks? You had so better not be trying to put me under some kind of spell."

He was across the room in less than a second. He grabbed her, pulling her against him. "I'm serious, Sara." He couldn't stand the thought of another seeing her smooth skin, her round breasts, her pale thighs… "Dammit, you're mine. *Mine.*"

She knocked his hands aside. "You don't own me, Fury. I belong to myself, got that? And if I want to dance naked in front of—"

"Me. Only me." A part of him knew she didn't understand the way of their kind, but rage was riding him hard. "He could smell you," he muttered.

Her brows snapped together. "Not that crap again."

He opened his mouth to reply, determined to make her listen to him, but then she sniffed, and Torian thought he saw the edge of a tear on her lashes.

The anger left him in a sudden rush. "Sara…" He swallowed. "You don't know what it's like for the men here."

"I know you're all jerks." The back of her hand rubbed against her cheek. "That's what I know."

How could he make her understand? A mate close to the Becoming could drive a wizard nearly insane with jealousy because there was always the fear that she would choose another, that she would deny the destiny that waited for her. Deny the wizard that waited.

"Sara, when the Becoming is close..." He hesitated.

She rolled her eyes and pushed past him. "Don't start that again."

"No, wait!" He touched her shoulder.

One golden brow arched as she glanced back at him.

"You have to understand. Wizards...we can lose control. And that can be very, very bad. A mate is the most important thing to us, and if we think she's being threatened, or if we think we may lose her..." He broke off, remembering the broken wizards he'd seen in his life. The empty shells who'd lost their mates before the Becoming. "We lose control."

She cocked her head to the side. "What do you mean?"

"Becoming is forever. Mating is forever. And if we think something, or someone, will threaten that..."

"What do you do?" Her voice was hushed.

"We fight. We kill." Theirs was not a civilized society. Too much of the darkness remained in them all. "Nothing comes between a wizard and his mate. Nothing."

Her eyes, so wide and blue, met his. "I-I see."

But he didn't think she did. Not really. He would never hurt her. But if someone tried to take her from him, he would show no mercy. "No man will take you from me," he growled. "No one can take you." He took a deep breath. "Don't confuse me with your mortal men, Sara. I'm different, far different, from their kind."

He stroked the smooth skin of her shoulder. "Those sparks that you saw a moment ago. You see them when my emotions are high...or my passion is aroused. They won't hurt you as they are. They won't hurt anyone. But if I were to lose my control, if you were to ever be threatened, the sparks would turn into flames, and the flames would destroy everything around me."

Her lips parted on a startled gasp.

"I'm not a mortal. I won't ever be." And his strength, his power, was deadlier than a mortal could ever imagine. "And you are far different from a mortal woman."

Sara shook her head, and he easily read the denial on her face.

"No, it's true. Lie to yourself if you must, but I know. I know *you.*"

He turned away from her. "There are clothes in the bathroom for you. Dress, then come downstairs. We have much to do."

"Please."

He stopped and looked back at her. "What?"

Her jaw was locked. "Why don't you try saying 'please' next time? Trust me, asking nicely with me works better than giving orders."

Heat rose in his cheeks. "I didn't realize." He cleared his throat. He was so used to giving orders that it was second nature to him. "Will you *please* get dressed and come downstairs?"

"Yes, I will." Her lips pursed. "Now really, Torian, was that so hard?"

He growled and jerked open the door. Her laughter followed him down the hall.

* * * *

Sara took her time dressing. Normally, she could have put on her clothes and been downstairs in less than three minutes. But she rather liked the idea of Torian waiting on her. Served him right.

And you are far different from a mortal woman. His words kept playing through her mind, like some damn broken record that she couldn't stop.

And the really annoying thing was…she knew he was right. She was slowly discovering that she *was* different. Very different.

Her old life was gone, and Sara knew she'd never get it back.

The clothes he'd laid out for her were certainly not what she'd expected. She found a pair of sheer black panties and a matching bra, and she pulled them on quickly, surprised by their softness against her skin. There was also a pair of black leggings that clung tightly to her thighs. A bit too tightly for her taste, but it wasn't as if she had a lot of options.

He'd also left her a black shirt with a scooped neck and long, flaring sleeves. The shirt was made of the same soft, supple material as Torian's pants.

And on the bathroom floor, she found a pair of boots and

some thick, black socks.

Apparently, the man had thought of everything, and for some reason that irritated her.

When she could delay no longer, she marched out of the bathroom and headed for the door. She turned the knob and then carefully poked her head out, looking to the left and then to the right.

The hallway was deserted. Good. That gave her a little time to snoop around.

Her footsteps were cushioned by the thick carpet, so she made no sound as she walked. There were a dozen or so rooms connected to the hall, and a quick scan showed her that they were bedrooms with heavy wooden furniture and very, very large beds.

The hallway was lit by a line of gleaming white orbs that hung just inches below the ceiling. She'd found more of those orbs in the bedroom, hidden beneath lamp shades.

But then, Torian had already told her that technology wasn't used much on his world. No, on Taren, magic was the way to go.

Damn. Things were going to be different for her. So very different...

At the edge of the hallway, she found herself at the top of a curving staircase. She could hear voices, the words drifting up to her. She put her hand on the wooden banister and leaned forward, shamelessly eavesdropping.

"Your mate isn't what I expected." A man's voice. Strong. Hard.

"No, Sara's not what I expected, either." Torian's voice. She would have known that deep drawl anywhere.

She frowned. Just what did he mean, she wasn't what he'd expected? She inched down the stairs.

"She's beautiful." The other man was talking again, and she recognized his voice. It was the Peeping Tom who'd popped into the bedroom earlier. What was his name? Fabio? No, Fabian. Yes, that was it. Fabian.

"I could smell her power," Fabian said.

Her nose wrinkled.

"The Becoming is close. In three more days, I will claim her." There was a sudden edge to Torian's voice. "And no one will come between us."

"Relax, Fury. I know she's yours."

"Good. Don't forget it." A pause, then, "I'd hate to have to kill you."

Silence. She gulped. Okay, Fury had just threatened to kill a man. What the hell was that about?

"She's not interested in me." Fabian's tone was softer now. She strained to hear him. She hurried down a few more steps. "She only has eyes for you. I could see her hunger for you, her desire."

Sara flushed. Damn. Was she that obvious? Could even a stranger read her now? She slid down another step, and the stair creaked loudly beneath her foot. She winced.

The men stopped talking. She closed her eyes for a moment, wishing she had the power of invisibility.

But, hell, currently, she didn't even have the power to make a good fire. Sighing, she opened her eyes and saw Torian staring up at her. One black brow was arched.

"Eavesdropping, Sara?"

She widened her eyes, hoping she looked innocent. "What? I was just walking down the stairs, trying to find you." *And I decided to stop and listen to you talk to your good buddy.*

"Um." He looked doubtful. "Come on down then, I want you to meet Fabian." He paused, winced and said, "Properly meet him, that is."

She hurried down the last few steps. "Whose place is this?"

He took her elbow and steered her to the right. "Mine. It's my home."

Her eyes widened. The place was huge. They were walking past a fireplace, and she could see a dining table in the next room. The table had to be at least twenty feet long. "Uh, how many people live with you?"

"No one lives with me."

She blinked. He had to be kidding. A house this big and he lived alone?

"Well, Daylon lives out back. But I don't let him in the main house. That would be too dangerous."

"And Daylon is...?"

"My dragon."

Her breath exhaled in a fast whoosh. "Right." She swallowed. "Your dragon. I should have known." Like she really believed that.

"Don't worry, I'll introduce you to him soon."

Oh, damn. He was serious. "You...really have a dragon?"

"Of course. All wizards train with dragons here."

Great. Just great. She'd get to meet his pet dragon, and hopefully, he wouldn't decide to eat her.

They entered a circular room. A large crystal ball sat on a marble table in the middle of the room. Fabian stood next to the ball, and when he saw them, a smile slipped across his lips. "Hello, Saralynn." He bowed before her.

"Uh, you can just call me Sara."

He glanced up at her and a lock of blond hair fell across his forehead. "I am Fabian le Knight. You may call me Fabian."

He flashed that smile again, and Sara's breath caught. My, they really did grow them handsome here. Fabian was like a tall, blond, surfing god. He had wide shoulders and muscular arms and a smile that could easily turn a woman's head.

But the strange thing was, she didn't find herself attracted to him. He was cover model perfect, but when she looked at him, nothing happened.

From the corner of her eye, she glanced at Torian's dark features.

Zing. And there it was. Just a look, and her body tingled. What had the man done to her? A lust spell?

She shook her head and focused her attention back on Fabian. "Are you a wizard, too?"

He nodded.

Her eyes narrowed in suspicion. "You're not one of those Dark wizards, are you?"

Fabian shot a quick glance toward Torian. "A Dark wizard?" He coughed. "Uh, no. I'm not."

"Good, because I'm really starting to hate them."

Beside her, Torian seemed to flinch.

Fabian coughed again. "Uh, yeah. I can understand why you might feel that way."

She shrugged. "When people try to kill me, it tends to upset me."

"Torian told me about the fire." His features hardened. "We'll find the one who did that, don't worry." He looked back at Torian. "When will you train her?"

Train her? Uh, oh. Was this more power training? She didn't know if she was up for that now. "Um, Torian..."

"We start now." He waved his hand and the doors on the left side of room swung open.

She tilted her head, trying to see inside. "Torian, just how big is this house of yours?" The man really needed to consider downsizing. No person could possibly need this much space.

He ignored her question and asked Fabian, "Can you help?"

Fabian nodded.

"Good. She's going to need all the help she can get."

"*She* can hear you," Sara snapped, glaring at him. And the last thing she wanted was to practice magic again. What if she burned down Torian's beautiful home?

"You can tap into your power now," Torian said, turning to fully face her. "Back at the cabin, I opened a gateway—a door—inside your mind to your power. That was why you were able to start the fire."

"Yeah, and that door you opened led to a huge fire that destroyed the cabin." She took a quick breath. "I can't control the power. I can't make it stop." The admission was hard.

He took her hands, rubbing her wrists lightly. "You can control it. You *will* control it." His lips curved downward. "That fire wasn't your fault. I told you—"

"I know. The Dark One. " But she still felt responsible. She'd called the fire. She should have been able to force it back down once the dark wizard took control. But she'd been powerless. And utterly terrified.

"You have more untapped power than any witch I've ever met." He was ignoring the avidly watching Fabian and focusing completely on her. "When we mate, when you Become, you will be unstoppable. Your full power cannot be matched."

She didn't know what to say. She got that he thought she was some kind of super witch, but she didn't feel super. She just felt...scared. What if she couldn't do it? What if, no matter how long Torian trained with her, she just couldn't use the magic?

She would be a failure, again.

And their worlds would be screwed.

Her gaze darted toward the open doors and the dark room that waited for her.

"I know you can do it," he whispered.

And she knew she had to try. She couldn't just give up. Not with so many lives on the line. She nodded. "Okay." Exhaling on a hard breath, she muttered, "Let's go."

Sara marched toward the room, wondering what waited for her. And she wished that her knees would stop shaking.

* * * *

"Torian, are you sure about this?" Fabian asked, holding up the wickedly sharp blade. His shield marking was visible on his right wrist. His tattoo was identical to Torian's.

Hmm. Sara frowned, her attention immediately captured by the shield design.

"Yeah, I'm sure, I—"

Sara grabbed Fabian's hand, carefully avoiding the gleaming blade. "So, are you another Guardian?" Her fingers tapped against the black marking.

Fabian nodded.

Great. So she had another all-powerful Guardian wizard on her hands. "Sworn to protect witches, huh?"

"The few that are left." And there was sadness in his eyes. A deep, haunting sadness.

Sara dropped his hand and stepped back. "I-I'm ready whenever you are."

Fabian swallowed and his head bowed for a moment. Then he looked back at her, and his expression was blank. "Do you know what you have to do?"

"Yeah." Unfortunately.

"Just focus, Sara," Torian said, moving to her side. "Focus like you did with the balls earlier."

The magic with the balls had been surprisingly easy. She'd made those little babies dance around the room. But balls and knives, well, they were two completely different things. She glared at him. "Fury, making a couple of rubber balls dance in the air is one thing. Stopping a knife before it lands in the middle of your chest is a whole different ball game."

And she thought it was a really, really bad idea. She'd told Torian that about ten times, but the man just kept ignoring her.

She licked her lips. "Ah, tell me once more why he can't just throw one of those nice bouncy balls at you? I know I could stop that before it landed."

"You aren't afraid of the balls." He pointed toward the knife. "That scares you."

Yes, sharp objects did scare her. Especially when they were flying through the air. And since Torian had finally told her the story behind the *Knias,* the knives that all Guardians used, she was really, really scared. Apparently, once wizards went dark, they became extremely hard to kill. And only weapons created of magic, like a *Knias,* could destroy them.

"You have to face your fear." Torian stroked her shoulder,

a quick, gentle caress. "If you control your emotion, you control your power."

Fabian lightly tossed his blade into the air. "It's the first rule of magic. Never let emotion rule you."

"Because if it does," Torian said, "it can blind you, overwhelm you. Destroy you."

Fabian tapped the blade against his leg. "Fear. Anger. Love. They'll cloud your judgment, make you weak."

Torian's gaze met hers. "You have to block them out, Sara. You have to be able to block everything out."

"But what if I miss?" The blade was so sharp. *Too* sharp. "I can't do this. I don't want you hurt." And she didn't. She might want to scream at the man for yanking her out of her world without permission, but she didn't actually want Torian hurt.

His lips hitched up in a half-smile. "Don't worry about me."

Fabian laughed softly. "Relax, witch. If you miss, I'll be here." He pointed toward Torian. "There's no way I'll let it hit him."

Well, hell, he should have just told her that to begin with! Sara exhaled heavily, feeling relief sweep through her. There was a backup plan. She really liked backup plans. "Just to be clear, Torian isn't in any danger?"

"Don't worry," Fabian assured her. "I'll watch the blade."

"Okay." Then she would do it. "I'm ready."

Torian paced across the room. "Remember what I said. Don't focus on moving the knife itself. Call to the wind. Let the wind move the knife, just like you used it to move the balls."

"Right." Her palms were sweating.

Fabian lifted the *Knias*. It was a knife much like the one Torian wore, but its hilt was completely encrusted with diamonds. "Torian?"

He took his position beside the back wall. His gaze met hers one more time. "Just remember to focus."

She nodded.

Fabian drew back his hand and the knife shot through the air, spinning end over end in a flashing blur.

Wind. Wind. She stared at the knife, focusing her strength, all of her energy on that spinning object.

A breeze blew through the room, ruffling her hair, but the knife kept spinning, heading in a deadly arc toward its target.

Stop. She needed the knife to stop. Needed the wind to lift it away. She raised her hand—

The knife flashed and the diamonds sparkled. Then it froze. Less than a foot away from Torian's chest, it froze in midair.

And all of the air left her lungs in a stunned gasp. She'd done it! She'd actually done it!

A smile split Torian's face.

She ran across the room and threw her arms around him. She heard a soft clang as the knife dropped to the floor. "I did it, Torian! I did it!" She was flushed with success and so damn giddy that she felt like she was going to bounce out of her skin. "I stopped the knife!"

His arms wrapped tightly around her. "I knew you could do it."

Yeah, he had. He'd said from the start that she could do it, that she could use her magic. But until this moment, she hadn't believed she would have the control.

Sara cupped his face in her palms and, thrilled by her newfound power, leaned forward and kissed him.

She'd meant for the kiss to be light. To be brief. But the moment her lips touched his, everything changed.

His mouth met hers. Open. Hot. And she felt the slide of his tongue. She forgot about being light, about being brief. And she just thought about how good he tasted.

She felt his fingers sink into her hair, felt him tilt her head back. And she felt his arousal, strong and hard, pressing against her stomach.

"Ahem."

She ignored the sound and stood on tiptoe to better reach Torian. He growled low in his throat, and his tongue thrust into her mouth.

"I said, 'ahem.'"

Her eyes snapped open and she jerked away from Torian. She whipped around to find Fabian watching them, his arms crossed over his chest.

Heat rose in her cheeks. What must that man think of her? First, he'd walked in and seen her naked in Torian's bedroom. And now, well, she'd practically attacked Torian right in front of him!

Torian touched her arm, holding her when she would have hurried away.

"Um, well, maybe we should get back to training." She tried to keep the tremor from her voice and failed.

Torian stroked her skin. Then he leaned forward and gave her a hard, quick kiss of possession.

Her knees did a little shimmy. And so did her heart.

He stroked her lower lip with his thumb. "We'll finish this," he murmured too softly for Fabian to hear. "Later. When we're alone."

There was a promise in his words.

She shivered, wondering what the night would bring. Suddenly, training didn't seem nearly as exciting as it had before. Not nearly as exciting as being with Torian. In his arms. In his bed.

"Tonight," he whispered. "There is much I will show you." His gaze was heated as it swept over her body. "Much I will do to you."

She gulped. "But I didn't think we...could." She glanced quickly over at Fabian, hoping he couldn't hear her words.

"There are other ways," Torian told her. "And I will show them all to you...tonight."

Tonight. For the first time in her life, she couldn't wait for darkness to fall.

Eight

She expected to share a bedroom with Torian. She expected to lie naked with him throughout the night. But after dinner, he disappeared and Fabian escorted her back up the stairs and to a room at the end of the hall that she'd never been in before.

"Here you go." Fabian swung open the door.

"Thanks." She brushed past him and entered the large bedroom. A heavy four-poster bed sat in the middle of the space. It was covered with white pillows and what looked like white satin sheets. She saw a cherry wood dresser to the right, and there was an old bookcase in the corner.

And there was no sign of Torian.

Fabian motioned toward a white door and then waved toward a hanging curtain. "That's your bathroom, and over there is your closet. There are plenty of clothes inside for you."

"Who got the clothes for me?" She asked, curious.

"Torian did."

Oh. A warm glow spread through her. "And where is our dear Torian right now?"

Fabian raised a brow. "Missing your mate already?"

Sara flushed. "Look, he said we were supposed to meet, okay?" Not that it was any of Fabian's business, anyway. And she certainly wasn't going to tell the blond lug that she and Torian had personal business to attend to. *There is much I will show you. Much I will do to you.* A shiver ran down her spine.

"He had to leave." Fabian turned on his heel and headed for the door.

"What?" She blinked. He'd left? But he was supposed to come to her, supposed to—

"A missive arrived." Fabian pulled open the door.

A missive? Was that like a note? "And what, he just took off?"

"Yes." Fabian walked out of the room.

She ran after him. "He left?" she repeated, her voice rising an octave. "He just left?"

He glanced back at her, his face grave. "He had business to attend to."

Right, business. Important business, no doubt. Probably some stupid wizard issue. So much for their plans. Apparently, she didn't even rate a good-bye.

"He stood me up," she muttered, pinching the bridge of her nose. "The jerk stood me up."

Fabian frowned. "He had to go."

"When did he get this missive?"

"The messenger arrived right after dinner."

Her gaze narrowed. "Do you know what the message was about?"

A cautious nod.

Curiosity began to burn within her. What was so important that Torian had run out into the night? "Are the wizards rebelling or something? What's going on?"

He hesitated, looking ill at ease.

"Come on," she urged. "You can tell me." What had happened?

"Torian will return soon."

Well, that was great to know, but it didn't answer her question. Where had he gone? And why? "Is it…another woman?" The words were hushed, and the moment they left her mouth, she wished that she could call them back. She hadn't meant to say that, truly she hadn't. The words had just…tumbled out.

"No." Fabian's voice was nearly as soft as hers had been. "You are his mate. For him, there is no other."

Doubt nagged at her. "But I'm not his mate, not yet." Why was she telling him this?

"You will be." Turning on his heel, he marched down the hallway.

"Wait!"

He froze.

"Tell me, why did he leave? Is everything all right? I mean, Torian's not in danger or anything is he?" She tensed, waiting for his answer.

"It's good of you to be concerned for him." He didn't look back at her as he made this pronouncement. "But you have no reason to fear. Torian can take care of himself."

"Everyone needs help sometimes," she muttered, glaring at his muscled back. Torian was strong, but he wasn't invincible. No one was.

Fabian swung around to face her, a bemused expression on his face.

"Well, it's true," she said. "You guys are hell on wheels with magic, but you're not unstoppable, you know."

"Yes, I know." And she saw that same strange flash of sadness fill his eyes again. "Wizards can die, just like mortals."

"And here I was, thinking you guys lived forever."

"No." He shook his head adamantly. "Just for about three hundred years."

Her jaw dropped.

The sadness vanished from his gaze. His lips curved. "Don't worry. When you Become with Torian, you'll live that long, too." He sighed. "Now go to bed, Saralynn. Torian will come back to you soon."

She held her ground. "You still didn't tell me why he left." No way was she just going to let this drop. There'd better be a damn good reason why Torian had bailed on her.

His lips tightened. "Well, I guess you'll learn about it sooner or later anyway."

"What is it?" Getting answers from this man was worse than trying to get a raise from her boss at the gallery.

"He found out that his father might still be alive."

Her breath rushed out. "What?"

"Torian thought his father had died years ago. But word reached him tonight that a Guardian on the outskirts of town thinks he saw him."

"But that's great! If his father is alive, then Torian must be thrilled." Oh, how often she'd wished that there had been some miracle in her own life, that she'd wake up one morning and that car accident would never have happened. That her mother would still be alive.

It seemed that Torian had that miracle. His father might be alive. How wonderful. Sara felt a smile spread across her face. And then she realized that Fabian was looking at her like she was crazy. She blinked. "What? What is it?"

"Torian hasn't told you?"

"Told me what?"

But Fabian was shaking his head and stepping back. "No, this isn't my place. I shouldn't have said anything."

She grabbed his arm. "You are *not* leaving." Not without telling her everything she wanted to know.

One brow rose. "Do you really think that you can stop me?" He sounded incredibly arrogant and just a little curious.

"I can try." Something was up, something serious, and she needed to know what it was. She could feel her stomach knotting, feel tension pounding through her blood. What secret was Torian keeping from her?

Fabian touched her cheek, a feather light touch. "You know, it's really too bad you were marked for Torian. You would have made one hell of a mate." His nostrils flared as if he were catching her scent.

Uh, oh. The last thing she wanted was for old Blondie to start sniffing her. The only one she wanted getting close enough to smell her was...well, Torian.

She realized that she was still holding Fabian's arm. Probably not a good idea considering the way he was suddenly eyeing her. She dropped her hold and settled for a simmering stare.

He sighed loudly. "All right, you would have found out soon anyway. It's hard to keep something like this secret." His lips twisted. "But Torian probably wasn't going to tell you until after the Becoming."

"What is it?" And here was a good point for her to remember for future reference...Fabian could not keep a secret.

"It's his father. Lazern. If the story turns out to be true, if Lazern really is alive, Torian won't be thrilled. He'll be furious."

"Why?"

"Because ten years ago, Torian thought he'd finally succeeded in killing the bastard. If he's still alive, it means Torian's about to have a hell of a fight on his hands."

Shock swept through her. "Torian...tried to kill his own father?"

Fabian's gave a quick nod, and his expression was hard, cruel. "It was what Lazern deserved. Torian should have killed the old man years ago."

Sara shook her head, dazed. What kind of world had she stepped into? "Why did Torian—" She stopped, unable to say the words again. But there had to be a reason. The Torian she was coming to know wouldn't just...kill. Would he?

"Because Lazern was a murdering butcher who thrived on killing witches."

Okay, good reason. "Torian's father killed witches?" *Witches burn.*

Fabian's hands clenched. His cheeks flushed. "He'd take their power and then watch them burn."

She closed her eyes. Oh, damn. This was not good.

"He killed my sister," Fabian growled, and there was so much pain in his voice. "Drained her power then lashed her to a stake and burned her so that he could take every single drop of her magical essence."

Her eyes snapped open and she stared at him in horror. "I'm so sorry! I-I didn't realize." His sister. Oh, God, how horrible. Burned at the stake.

"She was sixteen. Sixteen." He swallowed. "She was so pretty. Her hair was blond, with soft curls. She had the greenest eyes, just like our mother, and her smile…" There were memories in his gaze. "She could get me to do anything when she smiled."

"Fabian…"

"When I found her, there was almost nothing left. The fire had been too hot, too strong. And she was just…gone." He drew in a ragged breath. "Lazern took her from me. She was all that I had left. My only family, and he took her. He killed her."

No wonder Fabian wanted the guy dead. She shivered.

"If Torian hadn't beaten me to him, I would have killed Lazern. I would have made the bastard suffer just like he made my Marie suffer."

If Torian hadn't beaten me to him. "Is that why he did it? To avenge your sister?"

His lips compressed.

"Fabian?"

"Torian's reasons are his own. You wanna know them, ask him."

Damn. "Tell me this much, at least. Do you think his father is still alive?" Because the idea of that guy, Lazern, wandering around scared her.

His gaze stared into the past. She could see the grief and pain reflected in his eyes. "If anyone could beat death, it would be him." His hands clenched into fists. "The Guardian who saw him…his sister was attacked, a young girl, Bren, barely fourteen years old."

Oh, God. "I-is she all right?"

"For now. Her brother was able to save her." His knuckles were white. "But if it's Lazern, we haven't seen the last of him, not by a long shot."

* * * *

When Torian returned to the manor, it was far past midnight and the house was dark. Tension still pumped through him. The Guardian he'd spoken with had seen a man fitting Lazern's description near a recent witch attack.

The woman, a girl really, was only fourteen. She'd been outside with her younger brother when she'd been attacked. Luckily, the Guardian had been nearby. He'd rushed to the girl's side before her power could be drained. The attacker, a man with a white blond mane of hair and very pale skin, had fled in a shower of blue flames.

Torian had inherited his ability to use blue fire from his father. Blue sparks always accompanied his magic. He and his father were the only two wizards he'd ever known to use blue flames.

"Dammit!" He didn't like where this was going, didn't like that Lazern might—

"Well, hello to you, too." A light flashed on inside the library.

Torian blinked, his eyes adjusting rapidly. *"Sara?"*

The light encircled her like a halo. She sat cross-legged in the overstuffed chair in the center of the room. Her hand was still on the lamp.

She was wearing one of the gowns he'd bought her. It was thin and a dark blue. It dipped daringly low in the front to reveal the high curves of her breasts, and the silky material pooled over her long legs. He loved her legs. Loved that smooth, pale skin.

He stepped into the room. "What are you doing in here?"

She shrugged. The front of the gown dipped down another tempting inch. "Waiting for you."

He froze. She'd actually been sitting here in the dark waiting for him? "I didn't think you liked the dark." He'd learned about her fear, the first time he'd touched her mind. He'd seen Sara as a child, huddled next to a small night light. *Monsters live in the dark.* In her memory, she'd been too terrified to sleep, too afraid to close her eyes for fear that some horrible monster would come after her.

Now she really did have monsters after her. But he wasn't going to let the Dark Ones get her. He'd kill them all first.

"I don't like the dark. Never have." Her voice was firm. "But I thought maybe it was time I tried to face my fear. You know, ruling that fear being the first rule of magic and all." Her hand tapped the lamp. "Besides, if I'd needed the light, it was right here."

He nodded slowly. Damn, she was beautiful. Her eyes looked so blue, just like the sky at noon. Her lips were pink, soft, and he wanted to taste them so very badly.

"Did you find out anything tonight?"

That he wanted her. That he didn't think he could wait until the Becoming to claim his mate. That he needed her. That every time he saw her, he ached.

"Did you, Torian? Did you find out about your father?"

He stiffened. Fabian. His old friend who'd never been able to keep his mouth shut. The guy gossiped worse than the old crones who lived in the tower. "What do you know about Lazern?"

Her sexy mouth tightened. "Well, from the sound of things, the guy was a real bastard."

Yes, he certainly had been. "What did Fabian tell you?" She wasn't running from the room, screaming in fear, so that meant Fabian might have actually managed to keep some details from her. Good.

"He told me about Marie." She swallowed. He saw the slender column of her throat move as she seemed to fight for control of her emotions. "He told me...what Lazern did to her."

Marie. Sweet, smiling Marie. She'd always been hanging around Fabian, trailing after him. Laughing, dancing. Shining like a bright light.

And then her light had been extinguished. Her laughter had turned to screams. Screams that he could still hear. Screams that would haunt him forever.

"Fabian said that your father, that he—he burned her."

She stood up and rubbed her arms. The light shone behind her, and he could see the outline of her body beneath the gown. He could see her soft curves. Her breasts. Her hips.

And he could hear the fear in her voice. "He said that Lazern did that, that he b-burned witches."

He felt an ache in his jaw, and he realized that he'd been grinding his back teeth. He took a deep breath, forcing himself to relax. Sara knew much more than he'd ever wanted her to find out.

"Is it true?" Her gaze was locked on his, and he could read the plea in her stare. "Did he—"

"Yes." He wouldn't lie to her. Not about this. "He'd steal their power and then burn them." And there had been so many witches. So much death.

He closed his eyes, remembering his mother, remembering her screams. Damn Lazern. He hoped that bastard was burning in hell.

But maybe even hell had rejected him.

Torian felt a light touch upon his arm, and caught the faint scent of roses in the air beside him. His lashes lifted.

Sara was watching him, and she was close enough to hold. To kiss. *To claim.* Her hand was still on his arm, and he felt the heat of that touch in every cell of his body.

"Was he a...Dark One?"

Lazern had been much more than that. He'd been pure evil. He'd used the dark arts, used stolen power. He'd killed. He'd raped. He'd—

"Was he?"

He didn't want to talk about Lazern. Didn't want to let his darkness seep into the room with them. But he couldn't deny her. And he had to tell her about Lazern, because her very life might depend on the knowledge.

"My father was the first Dark One."

Her eyes widened, but she didn't speak. She just stared at him, a growing fear etched onto her face.

"He was the first to go after powers that had been forbidden to us. He used the dark gifts, and he stole any magic that he could find."

"But you said Dark Ones didn't have true mates. Does that mean your mother—"

"He forced her to complete the Becoming. He forced her to be his mate." Forced her to bear his child, because he'd wanted a child of magic. But he didn't tell Sara that. Didn't want her to know the truth of his origin. Didn't want her to fear him. "My mother hated him. Hated what he was. Hated the darkness in him."

"What happened to her?"

"She...died." Flames. Screams. *Torian!*

He felt a tremor slide through him. No, he wouldn't tell her about that. He couldn't. Because if he did, he would lose her.

"My father—" He stopped. "*Lazern* was unstoppable then. He began attacking witches. He was hungry for power and mad with the darkness. He would kill just for the pleasure it gave him." And he'd laughed. Laughed as he'd watched women burn. Laughed as he'd made his son watch them.

"Oh, God." A tear slid down her cheek. "I'm so sorry, Torian."

He stiffened. "You don't have to weep for me, Sara."

"Yes, I do." But she lifted her hand and brushed away the tears. "It must have been so hard for you, growing up like that, with…with a monster."

Memories slipped through his mind. He saw the blood. The death. The pain. *"Do you want to watch her die, boy? Do you?"* His father's laughter echoed in his ears, and he felt the sharp cut of a knife against his skin. He heard his mother's scream.

"It was hard." The way he figured it, living in hell was probably easier.

"You killed him," she whispered. "That's what Fabian said."

He gave a quick nod. His only regret was that he hadn't tried it sooner. If he had, maybe he could have saved some of those women. Maybe he could have saved Marie. Or his mother.

"Is he really dead?" She bit her lip. "I know you got some kind of message tonight about him."

"Yeah, I did." And he prayed that the Guardian was wrong. But he had a sick feeling in the pit of his gut. The Dark Ones had been gaining strength recently. They'd been attacking more. They had to have a leader. They had to have—

"Ten years ago, that's when you did it, right?"

He noticed that she didn't ask him how he'd killed Lazern, and he realized that she probably didn't want to know. And, hell, who could blame her? He wished he could forget. Grimly, he nodded.

"Why now? If he's alive, why haven't you found out sooner?"

"He would have needed…time. To recover. To regain his magic. His power." Because Torian had done everything possible to break Lazern, to destroy him. "If he did survive that attack, he would have been weak, almost…like a mortal." Because just before he'd plunged his knife into Lazern's chest, he'd used a spell on him. An ancient spell. A dark spell. *The spell of life.* And he'd drained his father of his power.

"Do you believe that he's alive?"

He wasn't sure. But he hoped, he prayed, that the bastard was dead. Because if Lazern was still out there, he would set his sights on the one witch who could fully restore him. The one witch left in the world who would have the power that he'd need.

Sara.

Her powers were awakened now, and she was growing stronger with every moment that passed. Oh, yes, if Lazern was out there, he would go after Sara.

"Torian, do you think he's alive?" Sara asked again, her eyes wide.

"I don't know," he said honestly. But a part of him was afraid, very afraid. Not for his own life, but for her. Because not only would Sara give Lazern his power, but she would also give him vengeance. If he hurt her, he would be able to hurt Torian, too. Be able to destroy him.

And Lazern would be so very hungry for his vengeance. Lazern would torture her, kill her, to punish his son.

Torian looked at Sara, at her soft features, her sensual lips. At the eyes that met his so unflinchingly.

His mate.

What would he do if Lazern came after her? Would he be able to protect her?

"It's all right." She pressed her hand against his chest. "Torian, whatever happens—"

He kissed her before she could finish speaking. He couldn't stop himself. The hunger, the need was too strong. He had to touch her. To taste her.

Her soft lips parted instantly. He felt her sigh, felt the warm touch of her fingers through the fabric of shirt.

His tongue thrust into her mouth, claiming all the sweetness that waited inside for him. He was so hungry for her, so very hungry. He needed her. Needed her more than he'd ever needed anyone or anything in his life.

And if something happened to her… If Lazern so much as touched a hair on her head…

Torian growled, jerking his head back. He stared down at her, breathing heavily.

"I want—" Her. Naked. Her smooth legs wrapped around him. He wanted to be buried in her so deeply he couldn't tell where he ended and she began.

His body was tight, heavy with arousal, and he wanted to yank up her gown and thrust into her body. Deep and hard. Until he couldn't think, couldn't feel anything…but her.

Her hands were wrapped around his neck, and she was pulling him back to her, back against her body. He couldn't resist her. Didn't want to resist.

His tongue pressed against hers, slid inside her warmth, and he knew he could get drunk from her sweet taste.

He could feel her breasts, could feel the stiff points of her nipples pressing against his chest. He slid his hands down her back and his fingers tightened around the curve of her buttocks, lifting her, forcing her onto her toes and pulling her up against him, tighter. Closer. Pushing her against his hard, aroused length.

He wanted to be inside her.

A moan rumbled in her throat, the sound tempting him, calling him. Why should he wait? Why couldn't he just go ahead and claim what was his?

His woman.

His mate.

She smelled so good. Her scent called to him, wrapped around him. His right hand clenched the silky fabric of her gown and began to lift it up. Up—

Torian wrenched away from her and swore. What the hell was he doing? He couldn't take her body now. If he did, then—

"Torian?" There was need in her voice. Hunger. "Has anyone…ever told you…" She was panting, her breath rushing out, "…that you can be…a tease?"

She was hurting. He could smell her desire. Her need. He reached for her. "I can satisfy you. I can—"

Sara knocked his hand away. "No, not without you. Not again." She glared at him. "I know I can be a selfish witch, but I'm not taking my pleasure again, not without you."

He blinked. Her hands were on her hips and her furious stare was probably meant to intimidate him. But, damn, she was gorgeous. And he really, really wanted to strip that blue gown off her body.

"There is…another way." But she would have to trust him completely. And she would have to surrender all of herself to him. Body, and mind.

Curiosity flared in her gaze. "You mentioned that before."

He nodded. Before he'd gotten the message from the other Guardian, he'd planned to go to her room. Planned to show her—

But that was before she'd known of his father. She might fear him now. Might not trust him.

"Torian? What is it?"

He touched her cheek, brushing back a strand of her hair. "We can't mate…physically. Not yet." Even though his body was aching for her. "But we can share pleasure with our minds."

Her lips parted on a breath of surprise. "What?"

His fingers stroked her smooth skin. "Dreams, Sara. Sweet,

wonderful dreams. We can be together in our minds. In our dreams."

Sara's body trembled. "I'd have to let you into my mind again?"

"Yes."

"Last time…" She wet her lips. "Last time, something happened to me. I felt—"

"I know." It had been her power. Awakening. Unleashing. He hadn't expected the strength of her magic. It had knocked him off his feet, stunned him. "But this time will be different. I promise. You just have to trust me."

She hesitated, and he could feel his heart racing. Would she do it? Would she trust him enough to invite him inside? Would she?

"Torian…"

He touched her lips, felt the soft rush of her breath against his fingertip. "Do you trust me?"

She stared into his eyes. And nodded.

"Then come with me." He dropped his hand and stepped back. "Come with me…."

She exhaled heavily. "Okay. But I'm warning you, this had better not hurt." There was caution in her eyes, and a trace of fear.

He took her hand, raising it to his lips for a quick kiss. "I promise, sweet witch, you'll know nothing tonight, but pleasure.'

He scooped her up into his arms, cradling her like the precious gift that she was to him, and headed for the stairs.

Nine

Sara clung tightly to Torian as they moved up the stairs. She wasn't sure what she should expect to happen between them and she was more than a bit afraid. The last time Torian had gone wandering through her mind, he'd ended up on the floor, out cold, and she'd ended up feeling, well, not pain, but...

Different. She'd felt different. Like the old Sara had been erased and someone new had been left in her place.

And this new Sara could start fires and move objects with her mind. All because Torian had tiptoed through her thoughts. What would happen to her this time?

They were at the top of the stairs now. Torian didn't even seem winded, despite the fact that he'd just carried her up an entire flight of steps. His arms were wrapped around her, and she could feel his muscles flexing as they moved.

What would happen between them? What would this dream world be like?

He'd said she would know only pleasure. And when she'd stared into his gleaming silver eyes, she'd believed him.

But doubt was starting to eat at her. She just didn't like the idea of someone else being in her mind. Even if that someone was Torian.

He stalked down the hall, moving almost silently toward her room.

Her heart pounded. The drumming seemed so loud, she wondered if he could hear the furious beat. It was just that she was so...nervous. So scared. She hadn't even felt this way on her wedding night.

Of course, she'd married an accountant, not a wizard. And they'd spent the night in a honeymoon suite in Vegas. Now, she was about to let a man enter her mind for...well...dream sex.

Dream sex. Now that was a phrase that you didn't hear every day.

Torian kicked the door shut and carried her across the room. He didn't bother to turn on any lights, and she wondered how he could see. It was pitch black to her, and a quick burst of fear shot through her.

His arms tightened around her, as if he sensed her sudden tension. "It's all right."

He moved unerringly in the dark, and in just seconds, she felt the soft cushion of the bed's mattress beneath her.

"Torian—" Okay, maybe she should tell him that she was nervous. That she was working herself up to a serious state of pre-sex jitters.

"Shhh. Just relax. I'll take care of you."

There was a thick note of satisfaction, of pleasure, in his voice that stopped her speech.

"You said you trusted me, remember?"

Yes, and she did. But she was still afraid. Not of him, not even of the dark at that moment, but of herself. Of losing control.

"Just close your eyes, Sara. I promise, there's nothing to fear."

What if she disappointed him? She hadn't been good enough for her husband, and he'd barely been half the man that Torian was. She already knew Torian was deeply sensual. What if she couldn't give him what he needed?

He kissed her. His lips were warm, hungry against hers. Desire burned through her. There it was again. Just one touch and—

Zing.

She wanted him. Wanted him with all of her being. The doubts began to fade, and her hunger grew.

"Just close your eyes," he whispered against her lips, "and let me have you…"

She closed her eyes.

He kissed her again, his lips pressing against hers, his tongue thrusting deep.

"You taste so good," he whispered, pulling back. "So damn good."

The bed shifted. She felt him slide onto the mattress beside her, but she didn't open her eyes. She was ready, waiting, for whatever came next.

And she would do everything possible to satisfy him. To give him the same pleasure that he'd given her.

He took her hand in his. His fingers wrapped tightly around hers. "Now, let go. Just let go…and come…to me."

An explosion of stars flashed behind her closed lids. It was as if her body was floating, rising up, going higher, higher into the night sky. Going up, straight up…into another world.

* * * *

"Torian?" She was standing in a rainbow-colored field of wildflowers. The sun shone down on her, heating her skin, and the perfumed scent of the flowers hung heavily in the air. And she was alone.

"Torian? Where are you?" Sara took a tentative step forward. What had happened? How had she gotten here?

She felt a touch on her shoulder. She spun around, her breath catching on a gasp.

Torian stood before her.

"Where did you come from?" He hadn't been there a second ago.

One black brow lifted, but he said nothing.

"How did we get here?" she whispered. "The last thing I remember was lying in bed."

"You still are." His lips curved. "But your mind's here with me."

She blinked. "What?"

"This is our world." He took her hand, his fingers caressing her skin. "Yours and mine."

"This is a dream?" No, it couldn't be. It felt too real. The colors were too bright. The sun was too warm on her skin. And she could smell the flowers. People didn't smell things in their dreams, did they?

And she could feel the ground beneath her. She could feel the wind blowing lightly against her. She could feel Torian, holding her.

No, this couldn't be a dream. Dreams didn't feel like this. No way.

"It's magic, Sara. Sweet, wonderful magic." He smiled at her and waved his hand in a flowing, graceful arc.

His clothes disappeared. They literally seemed to melt away.

Her gaze immediately dropped to his chest. And, damn, what a chest it was. Muscles rippled, flexed. Strong, hard muscles that her fingers itched to touch. Dark hair was sprinkled across his golden skin and veed down below his hips. Her hungry stare lowered a few more inches.

Oh, my.

If this was a dream, well, she didn't think she ever wanted to wake up.

God had been very, very good to Torian. She felt her body flush. *Very good.* His manhood was long, thick. The bulging head was dark, moisture glistening on the tip. What would it feel like, for him to thrust into her? To thrust that thick, aroused length deep into her sex?

He laughed softly. "Sara, your mouth's hanging open."

She snapped her lips closed and cleared her throat. "You're um…a little more than I was expecting."

His gaze dropped to her body. "And you're exactly what I've been wanting."

She glanced down at herself. Her nipples were pushing proudly against the soft fabric of her gown, almost as if they were begging for his touch, his mouth.

"We won't stop this time," he whispered, sliding closer to her. "We won't stop until we're both satisfied."

She swallowed, trying to ease the ache in her dry throat.

"I want to see you. Without the gown."

Her hands were shaking as she reached for the hem. She didn't know a clever trick to make her gown melt away, so she had to do it the old-fashioned way. But judging by the hungry look in Torian's eyes, she didn't think he minded. No, he didn't seem to mind at all.

She lifted the gown slowly, inch by inch. She felt strangely wild, standing in a field of wildflowers and stripping for her lover.

She'd never felt so sexual, so free, in her life. Normally, she would have balked at the idea of showing her body to a man under a blazing sun. But this time...This time she wanted Torian to see her. All of her, even if it was just a dream. Or maybe, maybe because it was.

Sara lifted the gown over her head and tossed it aside. The wind brushed over her skin, over her breasts, almost as if it were caressing her.

Now she stood before him, clad only in a pair of light blue panties. Her chin lifted, and she stared at him, waiting.

She didn't have to wait long. Torian reached for her, pulling her into his embrace. His touch electrified her, shooting currents of heat, of need, straight to her core. His hands were on her breasts. Plucking. Teasing. And his mouth, oh, his mouth, was licking her, sucking the delicate skin of her neck.

She rubbed against him, against the thick length of his arousal. *She wanted him inside her.*

Her breasts were swelling, aching. She loved the feel of his fingers against her. Loved his touch. He moved, shifting his body, and he took her breast into his mouth. His warm, wet tongue swirled over her areola, and she shuddered, closing her eyes.

He sucked her, drawing her breast into the hot cavern of his mouth. Her fingers fisted in his hair. Heat pooled between her thighs. She felt her body moistening, readying. And her knees started to shake.

"Torian, I-I can't stand—"

And then she was on the ground, cushioned by the wild flowers. Torian was on top of her, his hips pressing between her legs, his mouth on her breast. His hand slid down her stomach. Down, down to the soft material of her panties. She lifted her hips, needing to feel his touch. Wanting him to stroke her sex. To push his fingers inside her and ease the aching hunger she felt.

He lifted his head and licked his lips. His stare was bright with lust. God, he was truly the sexiest man she'd ever seen in her life. And he was hers. *Hers*.

If it hadn't been a dream, she would have pinched herself. But she was too afraid of waking up, too afraid of losing this wonderful paradise that she'd found. So, instead, she wrapped her hands around him and pulled him back against her, marveling at the steely feel of his muscles.

Torian's lips touched her other breast, and he paid it the same loving attention, his tongue swirling around her nipple. He licked. Kissed. Sucked. Drew her breast into his mouth. Sucked harder, deeper.

His hand slid under the elastic of her panties. His finger rubbed against her folds, parted her delicately, and then pushed inside her core.

She gasped. *Oh, yes, just like that.* One broad finger worked fully inside of her.

His mouth suckled at her breast. His finger withdrew.

"Torian!"

He shoved two fingers into her sex, pulled them out, and pushed them back, again and again. Working them deep into her sex. Her hips arched. Oh, God, it felt so good. So unbelievably good.

She could feel her climax coming, feel her muscles tightening around his fingers, feel—

His fingers slid out of her body. His head lifted.

She was panting. Her muscles clenched. And she wanted him to *finish* her.

His stare moved down her stomach, resting on her belly button. And his lips curved. "Have I told you how damn sexy I think this is?" His fingers touched her golden hoop. "Every time I see it, I want to…" He didn't finish his sentence, just lowered his head toward her stomach.

She felt the rasp of his tongue. Sliding against the hoop, against her skin. Her teeth clenched.

"But I don't want anyone else to see it, to see you." His words were growled against her. "Only me. Forever."

Hunger was ripping her apart. She pushed against his shoulders.

"What?" His head lifted, and for a moment, she could have sworn that she saw fear in his eyes. "Don't ask me to stop—"

Sara shook her head. "No, I-I won't." But there were things she wanted to do, things she wanted to do to him.

He let her push him onto his back. Then she straddled him, putting her knees on either side of his lean hips, and she looked down at him.

The raw desire she saw on his face took her breath away. There was so much need there, so much hunger. And it was all for her. *Her.*

She lowered her head, keeping her eyes locked on his, and she licked his nipple, one long, slow lick.

He shuddered, his body stiffening against her. She smiled, loving the little thrill of power that shot through her. Maybe she wouldn't disappoint him after all.

She opened her mouth and rubbed her tongue against his tight nipple. She lifted her thighs just a bit, and then pressed down against him. Oh, yeah, that felt good. His arousal pressed against her sensitive folds.

His harsh groan filled the air, and she began to kiss her way down his body. Slowly, inch by delicious inch. She licked his chest. Kissed his stomach. Nipped the skin at his abdomen. All the while, she could feel his body tightening beneath her. Thickening even more.

She slid down between his legs. His heavy shaft brushed against her, demanding and strong.

"Sara…" There was an urgency in his tone. A dark need.

Her fingers wrapped around his thick length. He felt so warm. So strong. She stroked him carefully, moving from the large base of his arousal to the sensitive tip of his erection.

"Again," he said, his voice husky, his face tense. "Touch me…again."

And she did. Her fingers tightened around him and she stroked. Slowly. Up, down. She felt his body jerk, and she lowered her head until her lips were just inches away from the heart of his desire. She parted her lips and kissed him, her tongue swirling around the tip of his arousal. Then she took him into her mouth.

He shuddered and called out her name. His fingers fisted

in her hair, and he began to move, thrusting into her mouth.

She relaxed against him, drawing his arousal deeper into her mouth. Deeper. She loved the way he tasted. Loved the way he felt.

"Enough!" His hands were on her shoulders, pulling her up. "I can't wait any more!"

And she didn't want him to. She wanted him to take her. She was flushed, her body heavy with desire.

He lifted her, and in a lightning fast roll, Sara found herself on the bed of wildflowers again, staring up at Torian's tense face. His legs were between hers, the thick head of his erection pressing against her opening.

"You're wet," he whispered, pushing lightly against her. "I can feel you, feel your heat coating me."

And she could feel him. Hard and strong. The head of his arousal slipped just inside of her.

His thumb slid between their bodies and rubbed against her, right above her tender opening. She closed her eyes, choking back a moan. His touch felt good, right.

He thrust into her, pushing deep, burying himself to the hilt.

Oh, yes...

"Sara?"

She forced herself to lift her lashes.

"Is it too much?"

She shook her head. "No, no, it's perfect."

He was holding his body still, and she could see sweat forming on his forehead.

"I don't want to hurt you," he whispered.

"You won't." She wrapped her legs around him and lifted her hips.

"You fit me perfectly. So tight. So damn hot." He bent down and licked her breast. "Like you were made just for me." He looked up at her and smiled. "But then again, I think you were." He pulled back and then thrust deeply. Again and again his thick length slid into her body.

Her muscles strained as she tightened around him. She could feel her climax coming, could feel the pleasure building. Higher and higher. Closer. *Closer.*

He grabbed her hands and pushed them over her head. His head lowered and he kissed her, a hot, open-mouthed kiss.

And he thrust into her. Harder. Deeper.

"Come for me," he whispered against her lips. "Let me

feel you come around me. Let me feel you!"

The world exploded into a flurry of bright blue stars. Pleasure pounded through her. Waves and waves of pleasure. Her climax shook her entire body as she screamed his name.

Dimly, she was aware of him. Aware of his strong thrusts. Aware of the sudden tightening of his body. She felt the hot splash of his orgasm deep in her body. And she heard him whisper her name. His arms locked around her and he held her tight, their bodies shaking in the aftermath.

She didn't know how long they stayed that way. It could have been a minute. It could have been an hour. Frankly, she didn't care. She was in Torian's arms, her body still tingling from their lovemaking, and she never, ever, wanted to move.

"You are, without a doubt, the best lover I've ever had." Her voice sounded like a frog's croak, but she figured the man deserved a little ego stroking.

He lifted his head and leveled a hard look at her. "And just how many lovers have you had?"

"Um...two." She smiled at him. "But you were the absolute best of the two." She stretched, feeling a delicious ache in her body. "You know, I can't help wondering ...if you're this good in my dreams, what will you be like in reality?"

He smiled and kissed her. "You'll find out soon. Very, very soon."

Her breath caught at the heated promise in his words.

"But in the mean time..." His gaze lowered to her breasts. "I think I want seconds."

Sara inhaled and felt his shaft, still buried inside of her, swell and lengthen.

He pushed against her. "Can you go again?"

"Oh, yes..." Already, her desire was building again, her hunger growing.

He licked her breast and began to thrust, and she wished that she could stay with him in her dream...forever.

* * * *

It was the sunlight that woke her. Streaming through the window, it fell directly onto the bed. The bright light was the first thing she noticed when she opened her eyes.

The second thing she noticed was that she was alone in the bed and still dressed in her blue gown.

"Damn." She closed her eyes, grimacing. That had been the absolute best dream of her life. The. Absolute. Best.

She exhaled on a forlorn sigh. And, now, she was awake.

Alone, and awake. Could life be any more unfair?

Sara rolled onto her side and pushed out of bed. Where was Torian? Why he hadn't stayed with her? It would have been nice to wake in his arms. To turn and kiss him.

Rising slowly from the bed, she winced at the aches in her body. Her arms lifted over her head and her back arched as she tried to work out the kinks.

Damn, but her body ached. Of course, she'd used some new muscles last night and—

Whoa! She jerked her arms down, a sudden thought startling her. Why was she sore? That had all been a dream, hadn't it?

But how could she be sore…from a dream? Sara marched to the door and jerked it open. "Torian!" Her voice was a near shout. "Torian!"

A door opened down the hall, and Torian walked out, a white towel wrapped around his hips. Beads of water gleamed on his chest.

"What is it?"

She gulped, watching one drop of water slide down his chest. Down to the towel and down to…

"Sara, what's wrong?" He paced toward her, stopping just a foot away.

She shook her head, glancing back up at him. His dark brows were drawn low and he was looking at her in concern.

"Last night—" She paused, cleared her throat delicately and said, "It was…just a dream, right? I mean, we didn't really make love, did we?"

He didn't answer her.

"Torian?"

"It was real to me." His gaze was direct, unwavering. "But if the question you're asking is did we physically make love, then no, we didn't."

"But..." She flushed, *okay, this was so awkward.* "I-I'm sore…in places that…well, I shouldn't be." Could this possibly get any more embarrassing for her? But if they hadn't physically made love, why the sudden aches?

"When we were together, did it seem real to you?"

"Yes." It had seemed like absolute heaven to her.

He nodded. "The magic was strong. It seemed real, and your body thought it was." He smiled at her. "Tomorrow I'll have to remember how…delicate you are."

She blinked, not understanding. "Tomorrow?"

"The moon will be full."

Okay. That was nice, but what did they have to do with—

Uh, oh. She gulped. The Becoming. "Oh, my, is that tomorrow?"

He cocked one brow.

The Becoming. "Um, yeah, about that—"

"Don't be afraid." He touched her cheek, his gaze tender. "I'll take care of you."

But he'd mentioned something about pain before. She really didn't like pain. Her current aches were about as much pain as she could comfortably handle. "Just how much will it hurt?"

He gave her a quick, hard kiss. "Don't worry. I'll give you so much pleasure when I join your body with mine that you'll forget any discomfort you feel at the Becoming."

The guy sounded seriously confident. Of course, based on the previous night's performance, he sure had a right to that confidence.

But she still wasn't sure about the whole Becoming thing.

It's me, Becoming you. It's you, Becoming me. That just sounded so...serious. "So, wait a minute. The Becoming, is that kind of like...marriage...for your people?" Because she certainly didn't remember Torian getting down on one knee and asking her to spend her life with him. In fact, all she remembered was him breaking into her house and telling her that she was in danger.

"It's not like your marriage."

Oh. Sara blinked at his terse words, uncertain if she was glad or sad that the Becoming wasn't some sort of permanent arrangement.

"Your marriages end too easily. Three, four years, and then people separate." His gaze was hard now. Piercing. "The Becoming isn't like that. It's forever. Once we bond, there will be no going back, for either of us."

There will be no going back. She took a deep breath. "Um, you know, where I come from, the guy usually asks the lady before they—they—"

He frowned. "What is it that you want? For me to ask you...to be mine?" He shook his head. "You are already mine. You gave yourself to me last night when you took me into your mind, into your sweet body. There is no going back now."

She crossed her arms across her chest and glared at him. "You know, I think we have a problem here." And she wasn't talking about the Dark Ones that were after them. "You can be an arrogant jerk, you know that?"

His eyes widened.

"And how many times do I have to tell you? I don't belong to you, I belong to myself."

"You would refuse me?" His voice was hushed and pain flashed across his face. "You don't choose to be with me?"

Of course, she chose to be with him. The man was sexier than a Greek god and he made her feel like the most desirable woman on Earth, er...Teran. And he'd already risked his life, twice, to protect her. She'd be crazy not to choose him. But, well, a lady liked to be *asked*.

"Have you ever heard of candlelight? Music? Flowers?" He just stared at her, a deep furrow between his brows.

"You will not be my mate?" His words were deadly soft. His hands were clenched. "You refuse me?" He asked again.

She stilled. She suddenly felt a deep, burning pain. Like someone was ripping her apart. Stealing a piece of her soul. Leaving her alone, empty, hopeless. The pain was blinding. It was—

Not hers. In a flash, she realized that the pain coursing through her body was Torian's.

"Why?" The word was stark. "I need you, Sara. I need you so much."

Okay. Screw the flowers and the candlelight. His pain was ripping her heart apart, and the hunger, the raw need, in his voice was more than enough for her. She wrapped her arms around him, holding tight. "All right, Torian, I'll stay with you. I'll be your—your mate."

His body was stiff. His fingers locked on her shoulders and he pushed her back, gazing down into her eyes. "Be very sure, witch. Very, very sure. Because once we Become, I'll never be able to let you go."

She still felt the echoes of his pain. Of his fear. She swallowed. "Torian, I'm not—"

Footsteps pounded up the stairs, and Fabian shouted, "Torian! Torian!"

Torian turned, placing his towel clad body in front of her. She stiffened, a trickle of dread running through her. Fabian was at the top of the stairs now. His face was flushed, his eyes blazing.

"What is it?" Torian asked.

Fabian didn't even appear to notice their state of undress. His gaze met Torian's, and she was surprised by the fear she could see in his eyes.

"She's gone."

"What?"

Who was gone? What was happening? Sara reached for Torian. His body was tense, his muscles like steel beneath her touch.

"Bren's brother went to check on her this morning. Her room was torn apart, and there was no sign of the witch."

Her eyes widened. *Bren.* The girl from last night. The one who'd been attacked.

"Alert all the Guardians. We're doing a full search." Torian's voice was hard, determined.

Fabian nodded. "Do you...think she's still alive?"

"I don't know." Blue sparks danced in the air. "But I'm sure as hell going to find out."

Fabian hurried down the stairs, his thundering steps echoing through the house.

Torian turned to face her, his face an implacable mask. "Stay here today. Don't leave the house at any time, do you understand me?"

"She's just a child," she whispered, "Would he really burn a child?"

"If it's Lazern..." His gaze was bleak. "Lazern wouldn't hesitate. Besides, it's not like he hasn't done it before."

She sucked in a sharp breath, horror flooding through her.

"I'm not like him," Torian gritted suddenly, his fingers clenching around her arms. "Whatever you're thinking, stop. I'm not like him. I wouldn't hurt her, or you. Ever."

How could he even think—Sara shook her head. "I know, okay? *I know*." Torian wasn't evil. She would have known if he was. He was strong and he was good. And she would trust him with her life.

He took a deep breath and kissed her. A quick, possessive kiss that left her lips tingling. And left her wanting more.

Torian stepped away from her. "I'm going to search for Bren. I'll be back by nightfall."

Bren. It was a nice name, she thought. *Bren.* A fourteen year old girl. A girl who could be dying. She was out there, somewhere in Torian's world, and she was probably terrified.

Sara lifted her chin, determination filling her. "I'm coming with you."

He froze. The fire in his silver gaze would have stopped a lesser woman. As it was, it made her knees shake.

"No," he said very definitely, "you're not."

Her jaw tensed. "Look, I get that you're the all powerful wizard here, okay? But I am not going to just let you boss me around and—"

"You will stay here." She could actually feel the heat from his glare, and those blue sparks circling them were really starting to get bright.

But she held her ground. "No, I won't." She wasn't going to stay there, all nice and snug, while that girl was out there facing death. "I want to help you find her." She *needed* to help him.

"No."

The man could be severely aggravating. "I'm not asking permission. I'm telling you." Her hands fisted on her hips. "I'm going."

His head cocked to the side and he studied her with sudden calculation. "I could make you stay, you know. I could put you to sleep again. You wouldn't wake up until I returned."

Anger shot through her. "And when I woke up, you can bet I'd kick your ass." She forced herself to take deep, calming breaths. "I know that you're worried about me, okay? But I can't stay here. I-I know what it's like for her." She could still feel the hot breath of the flames on her skin. "I *know*. And I want to help."

His face was still unyielding. But the blue sparks were dimming.

"Torian...just let me try to help. I'm supposed to be a High Witch, remember?" Her eyes narrowed as she studied him. "I *can* help."

"And you can die." Torian's words snapped like a whip. "If the Dark Ones get to you, they'll kill you."

A shiver slipped down her spine. "You told me the Dark Ones aren't out during the day." That meant she wouldn't be in any danger if she searched when the sun was high. "They can't get to me now. I'll be safe." *And I'm not planning on dying.*

His fingers cupped her chin. "I don't want to risk you. You're far too important."

Sara licked her lips. "I need to help her." She couldn't bear the thought of the young girl burning.

He stared at her in silence. One minute, two. Then..."Fine." A muscle flexed along his jaw and his hand dropped, fisted. "But you stay with me. Every minute. And when dusk falls, I'm bringing you back."

She nodded, elation sweeping through her.

"Every minute, Sara. Do you understand? You stay by my side."

"I will."

"And if we find her and it's too late…"

She didn't want to think about that. They would find the girl in time. They had to. "It won't be too late."

His lips compressed.

"It won't be too late," she repeated stubbornly. They'd find her.

Torian's expression reflected his doubt, but he said merely, "Meet me downstairs in ten minutes. The others will be assembled by then."

The others. The other Guardians.

"They'll know that your time is close," he continued. "They'll sense your Becoming. And when we hunt, if any Dark Ones are hiding close by, they'll sense you, too."

Her hand slid over her birthmark, pressing against it through the thin silk of her gown.

"And if the Dark Ones get your scent, they'll follow you back tonight."

The mark seemed to burn.

"Are you sure about this?" he asked, his gaze searching hers. "You'll be putting yourself in needless danger. I'll look for the girl. I'll take the other Guardians and we'll search the countryside. You can stay here, where it's safe.."

Where it's safe. So she was supposed to stay all nice and safe while some kid was out there, terrified, maybe dying? "No!" She drew in a deep breath. "I want to help." She needed to help the girl. Yes, she was scared to death of those Dark Ones. She could still hear their screams echoing in her mind. But she wasn't going to back down. She wasn't going to turn her back on the girl.

After all, shouldn't witches stick together?

She was going with Torian. And if that meant she had to face the Dark Ones, then so be it.

"Then let's get ready," he said. "We've got a witch to hunt."

Ten

Torian wished he'd forced Sara to stay at the house. He glanced over at her, saw the paleness of her skin, and frowned. Dammit, why hadn't he compelled her cooperation? He should have forced her to sleep and left her where he knew she would be safe.

But she'd looked at him with those big blue eyes of hers, and he hadn't been able to whisper the words of his spell. Hadn't been able to deny her. And now she was with him, on the trail of a stolen witch.

The other Guardians had smelled the Becoming on her. He'd seen it in their eyes, in the sudden tenseness of their bodies. And he'd seen the envious looks in their stares as they talked to him.

A wizard was lucky, *very* lucky, to find a witch to take for a mate. And Torian hadn't just found a witch; he'd found a High Witch.

He'd separated from the others, not wanting to have the men too close to Sara. Of course, she'd seemed oblivious to the tension between the Guardians. She'd smiled and chatted to them, introducing herself with a firm handshake. It had taken all of his restraint not to grab her and keep her locked to his side. With the Becoming so close, he couldn't stand to see her near other men, much less touching them.

But his control had held, and he'd managed, *barely*, not to make a complete fool of himself.

If he hadn't claimed her in their dream state last night, he knew he wouldn't have been able to tolerate the presence of the others. But the memory of their passion had still been with him. He'd remembered what it had been like to hold her, to caress her, to slide into her tight, wet heat. And he'd known that while Sara might be smiling at the others, her passion, her desire, belonged only to him.

"You know, this place really isn't so different from my world." Sara was gazing at the pine trees around her. "If it weren't for the fact that I saw a twenty-foot, green dragon as I was leaving your place, I would really think I was back in Virginia."

He felt his lips curl. Daylon had no longer been able to control his curiosity about Sara. When the search party left, he'd been waiting outside. And as soon as he'd seen Sara, he'd licked her.

And she'd screamed.

It had taken quite a bit of talking to convince her that Daylon hadn't been trying to see if she'd make a tasty meal. Instead, he'd just been showing Sara that he liked her. Dragons tended to lick people they liked.

And eat those they didn't.

"It even smells the same," she continued, inhaling deeply. "You can smell the pine, the flowers."

He nodded, keeping his watchful stare on her as she walked over to touch a rose bush. Their worlds were similar in many ways. But they were also very different. Dangerously different.

His village, Trinadar, was located in the mountains. There was plenty of space between the homes. No wizard liked to live too close to another. Their homes were made of wood and magic. They could withstand virtually any sort of attack or disaster.

She stood up, walking back toward him. "Do you think the others are having any better luck than we are?"

He shook his head. He'd been in mental contact with the other Guardians. They were searching the mountains, but so far they'd found no sign of the girl.

Sara's lips tightened, and she started marching through the brush. "We've got to find her."

He followed at her heels. He didn't tell Sara, but with every hour that passed, he knew the chance that they would find Bren alive diminished. Time was working against them. Already, the sun was beginning to sink lower in the sky. They'd been searching the woods for hours, and still there was no sign of Bren.

The heat of the day beat down on him, and sweat coated his body.

The warmth was taking a toll on Sara, too. Her clothes clung tightly to her. Her movements were slower now, a bit more sluggish, and lines of tension had appeared around her soft mouth.

He knew she was fighting to hold on to her hope. Fighting to believe that they'd find her.

Blade, an empathic Guardian, had told them that he felt Bren's presence near Trinadar. Unfortunately, he'd been unable to hone in on her exact location. So the Guardians had spread out, and they were searching the mountains one desperate mile at time.

But if they didn't find her soon…

"Torian!" Sara cried out, suddenly doubling over and clutching her stomach.

He was by her side in a flash. "What is it? What's wrong?"

She looked up at him, her face a mask of agony. "I-it hurts. S-so m-much."

Fear knifed through him. "Sara?" He scanned her body, but he couldn't detect any physical cause for her pain.

She cried out again, her face twisting. "I-it's r-ripping m-me apart!"

He grabbed her and wrapped his arms tightly around her, muttering a spell of protection. She shuddered against him, and he felt the spasms that rocked through her.

Fabian. Blade. Come to me. As he mentally summoned his two most trusted friends, he held Sara, rocking her in his arms.

Fabian immediately appeared before him, his face strained. He took one look at Sara and his eyes widened in horror.

Blade shimmered into focus next to Fabian. "Have you found the—" He stopped, his mouth falling open in shock.

Torian fixed his gaze on Fabian. "Do you know what's happening?" He could feel the taint of dark magic in the air around him. Damn, he'd known that he shouldn't have brought Sara. Known that he should have left her at home where she'd have been safe.

"I-I don't know." Fabian took a step toward them and looked helplessly at Sara's shuddering body.

"Give her to me!" Blade's voice was hard. "Now."

Torian's hold on Sara tightened.

"I can help her." Blade's arms were outstretched. "Give me the witch." Blade was a powerful wizard, second only to Torian. His strong features were tense with strain, and Torian suddenly realized that the other Guardian was experiencing Sara's pain, her agony.

Blade was a tall, muscular wizard with jet black hair and rough, harsh features. Torian had known him for more than twenty years, and he'd never thought of doing bodily harm to the man before.

But he did now. Because Blade was connected to Sara. Psychically connected to her, and that shouldn't be happening. Empath or no, he shouldn't have been able to connect with a

High Witch. Only her mate should have been able to do that.

Rage pulsed through him. Blade wanted her. He wanted to take her from him. His lips curled back into a snarl. His hands tightened around her.

Sara moaned softly, and twin trails of tears leaked from her eyes.

"She's suffering," Blade said. "I can stop the pain. I can help her."

Torian's jaw clenched. He couldn't allow Sara to hurt. Could. Not.

There wasn't a choice for him. He picked her up and carried her to the other man. Blade's arms wrapped around her body and he pulled her to him, holding her tightly.

Torian's hands fisted.

And Blade and Sara vanished in a swirl of gray fog.

His heart stopped, and he lunged forward, only to be brought up short by Fabian. The other man was holding tightly to his arm, pulling him back. Torian glared at his friend, vaguely aware that the air was lit with the burst of blue sparks.

"Trust him," Fabian ordered. "I know it's hard, but it's Blade. He won't hurt her."

But she was his mate. His. And she'd vanished, disappeared with another wizard. She was gone, and he felt her absence all the way to his soul.

"Trust him," he repeated, his tone fierce. "He knows she's yours. He won't—"

The sound of thunder rumbled overhead. The sparks began to turn into flames, and Torian felt his control slipping. He needed to see Sara, needed to have her back in his arms. Back within his sight. "He's linked with her," he gritted. "I can feel it. He's in her mind."

Lightning streaked across the sky. He needed her. *Now.*

The air shimmered. Blade reappeared with Sara still cradled in his arms. She wasn't moving. Her neck hung over his arm like a broken flower.

"*Sara.*" His gaze snapped up to meet Blade's impenetrable black stare. "*Mine.*" He reached for her.

Before he could touch her, she moaned softly, her lashes lifting. She blinked, staring up at Blade. "Uh, hello…there." She swallowed, seeming to realize that she was in his arms. Torian watched as her eyes widened.

"It's all right," Blade said, his voice softer than Torian had

ever heard it. "You're safe now." He looked back at the other
two wizards, his gaze steady.

Torian could feel the beast within him growling, struggling
to break free. She was in Blade's arms. The Becoming was
close. The other wizard had some sort of bond with her. He
could feel her pain, touch her mind.

"Could you...put me down?" Her voice was very polite.

Blade shifted his body, setting her on her feet.

"Thanks," she murmured and took a step toward Torian.
Then her legs buckled. Torian lunged forward, but Blade beat
him, grabbing her arms and holding her upright.

"Okay." Sara took a deep breath. "That didn't work so well."
She was even paler than before, and a fine tremor rocked her
body. "Maybe...maybe I need a new plan." Her hand rubbed
against her stomach.

Torian couldn't stand it anymore. He grabbed her arm and
pulled her away from Blade and into his arms. He held her,
feeling her heart race against his, and he buried his face into
the fall of her hair, inhaling her light scent.

"Torian, wh-what just happened to me?" She sounded
confused, lost.

He lifted his head and looked over her shoulder, glaring at
Blade. He hated that the other man had been in her mind. Had
touched that secret part of her.

"I had to," Blade snapped, his hands clenching. "Another
few minutes and she would have died."

He felt Sara jerk in his arms. "Shh." He rubbed her back
and sent as much energy and strength as he could into her body.

"Why didn't you tell me?" Blade muttered, his stare every
bit as hot as Torian's. "Did you think I'd try to take her from
you?"

No one would take her from him. *No one.*

"Dammit, don't you know how rare she is? How important
to our people? You couldn't keep it secret."

"We all know she's a High Witch," Fabian cut in, stepping
next to Torian's side. "That's no secret."

"Not that!" Blade glanced toward Sara. "She's an empath."
His gaze softened as it rested upon her.

Sara raised her head and looked at Torian. "What did he
call me?"

"An empath," Blade repeated, his jaw locking. "Dammit,
Torian, you know how rare it is to find a female empath!"

Her color was a little better now. She no longer looked like she would fall over at any moment, but Torian didn't release her. He liked the feel of her in his arms far too much.

"She can't be," Fabian whispered. "That's impossible. We've never had a High Witch who could be—"

"Who was her father?" Blade cut in, his voice sharp. "I already know her mother was a witch, but who did she mate with?"

"She can't be," Fabian repeated, looking stunned.

A frown pulled down the edges of Sara's mouth. Torian felt her body tense against his. Then she pushed away from him. He immediately wanted to pull her back to his side. Instead, he clenched his hands into fists. *So he wouldn't grab her.*

"I'm here, you know," she muttered. "It's really rude to keep talking about me as if I'm not right in front of you."

Blade flushed. Fabian just blinked, apparently still astonished by the other wizard's news.

"I know you, know exactly what you are," Blade whispered, the intimate tone of his voice putting Torian on edge. "And I just saved your life."

She glanced at Torian, as if for confirmation. He nodded, still not completely understanding what had happened to her.

Sara rubbed her stomach, grimacing. "What the hell was that, anyway? I swear, it felt as if someone was trying to rip me apart."

"You were feeling Bren's pain," Blade said. "You're an empath. That's what you do."

"No." She shook her head. "Trust me on this one, I don't. I don't go around feeling as if my body is being torn apart." She exhaled heavily. "That's just not a normal part of my day."

"I had to take you away. To force your mind to break the connection."

Sara's chin shot up into the air. "Look, I don't know what you're talking about, buddy. I'm not an empath."

His black eyes narrowed and his nostrils flared.

Her eyes widened in outrage. "What are you doing? You had so better not be sniffing me!" She stepped closer to Torian. "What is it with the guys here? You're all gorgeous as hell, but I swear you have the manners of dogs!"

Despite her angry words, a rush of warmth filled him. She'd come closer to his side. She'd moved toward him, not Blade.

He lifted his hand, sending a series of sparks shooting

toward the other wizard.

Blade jumped back, swearing.

A pleased smile curved Sara's lips. "Thanks," she murmured. "I'm really getting tired of everyone sniffing me." She glared at Blade a moment longer, and then the smile slipped from her face. "Is it true?" She asked, her brow furrowing. "What he said, is it true?"

Was she really an empath? He didn't know. He'd never met a female empath before. But Sara's magic was strong. Very strong.

"Sara, tell me about your father." Blade's voice was soft.

She frowned. "My dad? What do you want to know?"

"He was mortal," Torian snapped. "He couldn't have been—"

"Yes," Blade interrupted, his voice firm. "He could have. I've seen it before. Sara, did he sense things?" Blade pressed. "Emotions? Feelings?"

"H-he was a psychologist. He helped people." She swallowed. "Children. He worked with children. He used to say that he felt their sadness...that he wanted to make them happy."

"He had to be an empath," Blade said, sounding pleased. "Probably weak, but he had the power, and he passed it on to you. Just as your mother passed her magic to you."

"But I haven't felt anything like this before!"

"I opened the door to your power," Torian reminded her. "All of your power." And if she was an empath, that talent would have been awakened, too.

"Earlier today, I-I felt your pain." She took a quick breath and gazed into his eyes. "In the hallway. I thought it was because we were linked, but..."

She stopped, shaking her head, but he knew what she was thinking. Maybe she'd sensed his emotions because of her power. The power of an empath rather than their bond.

She was watching him, her gaze questioning. "Was I really feeling Bren's pain?"

He looked at Blade. The other wizard nodded.

"Oh, my God. That poor girl." She covered her eyes for a moment, shuddering. "Wh-what were they doing to her?"

"Taking her powers." It was Fabian who answered. His hands were fisted at his sides. His face twisted with rage. "They were draining her magic, ripping it from her body."

Her lips trembled. "We've got to find her," she whispered. "We've got to stop them."

"*You* can find her." Blade stepped forward. "You can feel her and that means you can find her. Just lock on her. Use your power and *find her.*"

"I can barely control my powers!" Sara yelled. She closed her eyes a moment, then muttered, "Look, I think I've really accomplished something if I can start a small fire." Her lashes lifted. "How the hell do you expect me to find a girl I've never even seen?"

"You have the magic. It's inside. Use it," he ordered. "Find the girl."

"I-I don't know how." She sounded miserable. "I-I want to, but I can't."

"I can help you." Blade raised his hand toward her. "We can link together and—"

"No!" A force of pure rage thundered through Torian. His power leapt, and it took all of his control not to unleash his magic upon the other man. "You will not link with my mate."

Blade glared at him, at them. "The girl's dying, Torian! I can't get a lock on her, not on my own. But if I link with Sara, I think we can find her." He swallowed. "Time's running out, and you know it. *We don't have a choice.*"

His jaw clenched. "Yes, we do." He pulled Sara back into his arms. "Link with me."

She blinked. "What?"

"Open your mind," he whispered, bending to kiss her lips, "and let me in."

"Torian…" Her voice was a husky whisper.

"Link with me," he said, lifting his mouth a breath away from hers. "Use my power. My magic. Use it, use me, and find the girl."

She shook her head. "But I don't know how!" There was frustration in her voice now, and anger. "I can still feel her, but I *can't* find her."

"Yes, you can." Blade was watching them, his stare intense. "Just focus on her. Call her name in your mind. Use your magic…and find her."

She swallowed and closed her eyes.

Bren. Torian heard her whisper the name, but her sweet lips never moved. He could feel her, feel the delicate touch of her magic in his mind. Feel her pulling his energy, his power.

He'd blocked his mind to her before. He hadn't wanted her to see his past, his shame. But she knew about Lazern now. She knew, and she hadn't turned away from him.

Her body shook as the magic poured through her. Her eyes flew open, burning silver instead of blue. "Bren!"

The wind howled. Power surrounded her, surrounded them. Her body began to glow, alight with a strange silver fire.

Then in a flash, the wind stopped. Sara's eyes were blue again. The shining light was gone. She blinked at him and her lips curved into a smile.

"I found her," she whispered. She shook her head in dazed wonder, and a smile stretched slowly across her lips. "I found her!"

* * * *

Sara led them through the forest, running over the rough earth and through the brush. She couldn't believe that she'd actually found Bren. That she'd actually been able to use her magic to find the missing girl.

But she'd just closed her eyes. Closed her eyes, touched Torian…and been flooded with power. So much power. So much magic. And she'd seen the girl. Seen her huddling in the dark cave. Seen the fear in her eyes. The knowledge of death.

But Bren wasn't going to die. They were going to save her.

"There!" she yelled, pointing toward the mouth of a cave that curved around the edge of the mountain. "She's in there." The cave was a few hundred yards away. So close…

Fabian glanced toward the sky. The sun was almost to the horizon now, hanging heavy and low in the sky. "We don't have much time," he muttered. "The Dark Ones will be ready to hunt soon."

"How many did you see?" Torian asked her. "How many were in the cave with her?"

She hesitated. She actually hadn't seen any Dark Ones. Just the girl. "I-I didn't."

Torian spun to face her. "What?"

"I didn't see anyone but her." Lying on the stone floor of the cave. A broken doll with a tear-stained face.

"That's not right," Blade muttered. "They wouldn't leave her alone."

"Can you sense her? Can you feel her now?" Torian asked.

Sara shook her head. She hadn't felt the girl in the last twenty minutes.

"Damn." He glanced back toward the cave. "I don't like this."

"Is it a trap?" Fabian asked, eyeing the dark entrance.

"Blade?" Torian looked at his friend with a piercing stare. "What do you sense?"

Blade's gaze was narrowed as he studied the yawning entrance. "The cave feeds into the heart of the mountain. Stretches for miles. There's darkness, miles of darkness." He sighed. "I don't know. They could be there, but…"

But he couldn't feel them, Sara realized. He couldn't feel them, just like she couldn't feel Bren anymore.

What was going on? Had the Dark Ones known they were coming?

"Stay here," Torian ordered. "I'm going in."

She grabbed his arm. "Not alone, you're not!"

His jaw clenched. "I have to. If she's there, I can't leave her."

"I'm coming with you," she said. She was not going to let him waltz in there without backup.

Torian shook his head. "I can't risk you." He inclined his head toward Fabian. "Keep her here."

Fabian's hands closed around her arms as he said, "I will."

She jerked against him. "Let me go!"

Torian motioned toward Blade. "Come on. Let's see what kind of party is waiting for us."

"Torian!" She yanked against Fabian's hold, but the man's grip was unyielding. *Dammit!*

Torian looked at her, and his gaze held hers. "I can't risk you," he repeated. "You're too important."

He was important, to her! "You'd better be careful, you hear me? You'd better come back without a mark on you!" That way, she could pound him senseless and not feel bad about it.

He stepped back and seemed to melt into the forest.

"Dammit, you'd better come back," she whispered, fear tightening her chest. "You'd better come back to me." Because if he didn't return, she didn't know what she'd do.

* * * *

In less than thirty minutes, Torian appeared, running toward her. His face was a tense mask. Blade was on his heels. And there was no sign of the girl.

Fabian's hands fell from her arms. She turned, gave him a

fuming glare to let him know that his actions would not be
forgotten or forgiven anytime soon, and then ran to meet Torian.
Sara threw herself into his arms, holding him tightly. His hands
came around her, and he held her to him, held her close against
his racing heart.

"Don't ever do that to me again," she gritted, lifting her
head to glower at him. "I thought I was going to go crazy waiting
for you!" Wondering if he was hurt. If he was dead. Her arms
tightened around him.

"We need to get out of here," Blade said, glancing toward
Fabian. "We don't have much time."

Sara looked at the horizon. For the last half hour, all she
had been able to do was wait, pray, and watch the sun set. It
was halfway past the horizon now. Soon, its red glow would
disappear completely.

"What about Bren?" she asked. They'd come back without
the girl. Did that mean—

"I'll tell you when we get back to the house." Torian's voice
was hard, and his gaze swirled with silver fire. With rage. "We
have to get back, *now.*"

She looked back at the black mouth of the cave. In her
mind, she could still see the girl, see her on the ground. See the
tears pooling in her eyes. "But Bren—"

"She's not there," Blade said, as Torian began pulling her
away from the area. "That place was a maze of tunnels. They
must have taken her out right before we got here."

Damn. She ached for the girl, for the pain that she'd
endured. "We can't just leave her. They'll kill her!"

"No, not yet they won't." Blade sounded absolutely certain.
His fingers were wrapped around a yellowed scroll.

"How do you know that?" She dug in her heels, refusing to
move. "We can't just—Torian!"

He'd scooped her off her feet and thrown her over his
shoulder. "I'm getting you away from the cave, *now.*" He began
to run, moving quickly through the forest. The other two men
were following on his heels.

"Torian! Let me go!" The world was passing beneath her
in a sickening blur. Her midsection was banging against his
stomach with every step he took. And she really, really thought
she might vomit at any moment. She twisted, trying to break
free of his hold. "Put me down!"

He ignored her and kept running. She closed her eyes,

unable to watch the blur of green beneath her anymore. She
was going to get him for this. First he'd left her alone in the
woods with the bodyguard from hell, and now he was carting
her around like she was a sack of potatoes.

Yes, he would pay.

She kicked against him. "Torian!" He grunted, and his hold
tightened around her legs. "I swear, Torian, if you don't let me
go, I'll—"

He stopped. She breathed a sigh of relief. "Thank you. Jesus,
Torian, I don't know what you were thinking, but—"

He pulled her off his shoulder and set her down in front of
him. His hands stayed locked around her arms in an unbreakable
hold. "Don't be afraid."

Uh, oh. She hated it whenever someone said those words,
especially when *he* said those words. Because it meant she damn
well needed to be afraid.

"I'm going to use my magic to take us back to the house.
You'll see a shimmer of blue light, and then we'll be home."
His gaze was intense, and in the depths of his eyes, she saw
that his rage was still burning brightly.

"You're going to use your magic?" She repeated. "What
does that mean?" A sudden thought struck her. "Are we flying
home?"

He shook his head. "No. We're not going in the air. We'll
just go from being here—"

"To being at the house," Fabian finished for him. "Trust
me, it's the best way to travel."

Her eyes narrowed in suspicion. "Is this—" Damn, what
was the word? "Um, like teleporting?" Because he'd mentioned
teleporting to her once before, that first night, when he'd nearly
scared her to death. But he'd said teleporting was hard, that he
only used it in emergencies...

Oh, God. Just what had happened in that cave?

He nodded, looking strangely pleased with her. "Yes, it's
teleporting. And we'll be home in less than twenty seconds."

She shook her head and tried to step back, but his hold was
unbreakable. "Look, I'm all for fast travel, but teleporting..."
She swallowed. "On Star Trek, folks had to be *really* careful
doing that, because if they screwed up, people's molecules went
crazy." Sara took a quick breath. "I do *not* want my molecules
going crazy, thank you very much. I think I'll just walk back."

"No." His lips thinned and he stopped looking pleased. "We

don't have time for that. I have to get you home."

She shivered. The sky was darkening, and she could feel something, like a cold wind, that seemed to be blowing through the woods.

"Torian…"

"I'm sorry." His fingers tightened. "But I have to take you home." He waved his hands and began to chant.

Blue lights circled their feet. As she watched, stunned, they began to rise, spinning around them, faster and faster.

His arms wrapped around her. "Don't be afraid," he said again. "You're safe."

The blue lights were all around them, burning so brightly that her eyes watered. "My molecules had better come out right," she gritted. "Or else you will be in serious trouble."

His lips brushed against her temple. "I promise, everything will be fine. If there was any risk to you, I would never do this."

So said the man who controlled the spinning blue lights. She closed her eyes, unable to watch the blur. "You know, I get motion sickness. Severe motion sickness." She took a quick breath. "And people like me weren't meant to travel this way." She couldn't ride on a Ferris wheel, much less go spinning through space.

"Just breathe, Sara. It'll be over soon."

She prayed he was right. And she held on to him. Held on tight.

A soft humming filled her ears. Wind brushed against her face. She opened her eyes, saw a world of swirling blue, and then darkness surrounded her.

* * * *

"It's all right," Torian whispered, his lips brushing against hers. "You can open your eyes now."

She opened her left eye and saw the fireplace and the couch. Oh, thank God. She was back at Torian's. Relief swept through her, and she opened her right eye.

Fabian and Blade were staring at her. She realized that her hands were clenching the fabric of Torian's shirt. Sara cleared her throat and took a quick step back, forcing herself to release her death grip on him.

Torian glanced at Fabian. "Call the others back."

"But Bren—"

"Call them back," he ordered.

Fabian shook his head. "We can't leave her, not when we know what they'll do."

Blade handed him the scroll. "I think you need to read this."

Fabian unrolled the parchment. He flinched, his eyes widening in horror as he read, and then he glanced toward Sara.

She frowned. "What is it?" Her stomach clenched and she took a step toward him.

At once, Torian moved, blocking her path. "Why don't you go upstairs? It's been a long day, you should rest."

Like she was going to let herself get distracted now. "No, I want to see...that." She pointed to the scroll.

Fabian's hand clenched around the parchment. "I-I think Torian's right. You should go upstairs now."

Obviously, they didn't want her to read the scroll. "What. Is. It?"

Fabian handed the parchment to Torian. "I'll go call the others."

Sara held out her hand. "Give it to me, Torian."

He shook his head. "Sara, you're tired. Why don't you—"

"I'm not some good little girl who's going to run off to bed when you snap your fingers," she muttered. "I want to see that scroll, and I'm not leaving this room until I do." The scroll was about Bren. She knew it. "Just let me see it."

Blade backed out of the room, closing the door behind him. Torian held her gaze, his fingers locked around the scroll.

"Torian..."

"Forget about it. Forget the damn scroll. Go upstairs, I'll join you as soon—"

Oh, screw it. She snatched the scroll from him. He lunged after her. "Sara, no!"

She sidestepped, barely managing to stay away from him. "Why don't you want me to see this?" He didn't answer. "Is it about Bren?"

A muscle flexed along his jaw. "I already told you, Bren wasn't in the cave. She was gone before we got there."

"But this was there, right?" She held up the scroll. "And it's a message, from them." Understanding filled her. "They want something, don't they?"

The slight flaring of his eyes was the only answer she needed. Her breath rushed out as she realized what was happening. "It's a ransom note, isn't it?" Excitement filled her. "If they want some kind of ransom that means Bren is still alive. If we give them what they want, then they'll let her go!"

"There's no way in hell I'm giving them what they want. I'll kill them all first," Torian growled.

Staring at him, at the rage she saw in his expression, Sara knew that he meant what he said. And that didn't make a damn bit of sense to her. She shook her head. Torian would refuse their demands? He'd sentence Bren to die? "Why? Why would you do that?"

"Because the price is too high," he whispered, closing his eyes. "I can't pay it. I *won't*." His hands were clenched into fists.

The price was too high? What did he mean? Her fingers shook as she unrolled the scroll. And her heart stopped beating as she read the words that had been scribbled across the parchment.

A witch for a witch.
Rowena's Circle. Midnight.
The witch comes alone or Bren burns.

Oh, hell.

Eleven

The rest of the Guardians returned to the house within the hour. They filed inside, their expressions bleak. They all knew that not finding Bren before nightfall meant almost certain death for her.

Furious energy pumped through Torian. He still couldn't believe that the Dark Ones had asked for his mate. That they had dared to leave the scroll for him. When he caught them, they would pay. With their lives.

He glanced across the crowded room. Sara was staring out the window, her shoulders slumped. She hadn't said anything since reading the scroll. He wanted to go to her, to take her in his arms and just hold her, but now was not the time. When the others were gone, he would hold her through the night, keeping her close to his heart. And tomorrow, when the sun set and the moon rose high in the night's sky, he would complete the ritual and she would become his. Forever.

Bren's older brother, a tall, fair-haired wizard named Zane, walked slowly across the room. His face was haggard. His hands clutched a small necklace. The others parted to make way for him as he crossed to Torian's side. "Is...is there any word?"

"We know where she was earlier. In a cave about fifteen miles from here." Torian's voice carried easily across the room. "When we got there, they had taken her away. There were tunnels there, miles and miles of tunnels." He lifted his hand, showing the scroll. "They left us this."

A murmur went through the crowd. All of the men were staring at him, their expressions tense. Sara continued to stare out the window, her arms wrapped around her stomach.

"They want a trade," Torian said, disgust and fury in his voice. "They seek to exchange one life for another."

Silence.

"What?" Zane looked both shaken and hopeful. "They will let her go if we give them another?" He straightened his shoulders. "I will gladly trade my life for hers."

Torian shook his head. "They don't want a wizard."

Zane's eyes widened in horror. "No, they can't—"

Fabian stepped to Torian's side. "They want *a witch...for a witch*."

And Torian watched as the hope faded from the young

wizard's face. Zane's lips trembled, and he fell to this knees. "M-my sister is dead," he whispered, stroking the ruby necklace.

The others stared uneasily at one another.

"No, she isn't," Sara said softly, still looking out the window.

Everyone turned to look at her. Torian tensed.

"I can feel her, I can feel her now." Her hand lifted and touched the pane of glass. "She hurts so much. And she's so scared." Her hand fell. "All she wants is to come home."

Zane's eyes widened. "What? You *feel* her? How can this be? How can—"

"She's an empath," Blade said, positioning his body protectively before her. "She's locked onto your sister, feeling her emotions, her pain."

"No, that's impossible!" Zane shook his head and stumbled to his feet.

Torian crossed the room. "Trust me, with Sara, anything's possible." He wanted to be by her side. He wanted to be the one protecting her, shielding her. He was fearful of Blade, fearful of the man he'd called friend. Because female empaths could mate with male empaths. They could bond. They could Become.

And while he knew in his soul that Sara was marked as his, he couldn't shake the feeling that something was going to happen. That she would be taken from him by another. And he would trust no other man with her, not even his friend.

His fingers skimmed down her shoulder, and she turned to face him. There were tears in her beautiful blue eyes as she whispered, "I can't let her die."

Her pain tore at his heart. "We'll search for her. We'll find her, and—"

"No." She shook her head. "You won't find her. Not until she's dead. Burned." A tear tracked slowly down her cheek. "And I can't let that happen." Her chin lifted. "I *won't* let it happen."

He didn't like the sound of this. A lick of fear slid through him. "Sara…" There was a warning in his voice.

A warning she obviously ignored, because she pushed past him and faced the others. "I'm going to make the trade."

At her words, a rumble went through the crowd.

"No!" He grabbed her arm. "You aren't." He would not allow her to take such a risk. He didn't want the Dark Ones close to her, didn't want them to so much as look at her.

Her gaze met his, unflinching. "If I don't, she dies."

And what will I do if you die? he asked her, using their psychic bond to communicate. She didn't like it when he touched her mind without permission, but he didn't really give a damn at that moment because he sure as hell didn't like it when she wanted to risk her life.

Sara didn't answer him.

I won't risk you. I won't send you to your death! He would not stand helplessly by and watch her walk to meet the fire.

One of the Guardians called out, "She can't go! We cannot risk her!"

Damn right they couldn't!

"She's our future. The price is too high," another growled.

"They seek to weaken us by taking the High Witch," an older Guardian snapped. "We cannot fall for their tricks."

Then Zane stepped forward and the men fell silent. He paced across the room toward Sara. His movements were slow and measured, as if he carried a heavy burden upon his back. He stopped in front of her, staring deeply into her gaze.

"I love my sister," he told her, his words soft. "She is my family. My blood. I would give my life for her in a minute." He shook his head. "But I can't ask that of you."

"It's my choice," she said, her voice steady. "My life."

"No," Torian growled, moving closer to her. "It's our life." Their life together. The life they would have. The future they would share.

"We need you," Blade told her. "We need your power to defeat the Dark Ones. You're the only High Witch left, the only one with enough magic to fight against them. If we were to lose you…"

Then they'd lose the battle. Sara's magic, the magic of a High Witch, was unmatched. If they hoped to beat back the darkness, they would have to use her power. Use her.

And if they just handed her over to the Dark Ones…

"All would be lost," Fabian said. He shook his head. "No, the price is too high." There was grief in his voice, and Torian knew he was already mourning for young Bren.

The men nodded, all seeming to realize the truth. The Dark Ones wanted a devil's bargain. They wanted Sara, wanted her life, because they knew that she could help defeat them.

"You can't go," Torian rasped. "I won't let you." There would be no more talk of a trade.

There was a murmur of agreements from the men.

Sara shook her head, sending delicate strands of blond hair sliding across her cheeks. "Gentlemen, I think you're overlooking something very important." Her hands lifted, swiping at the tears that glistened on her cheeks.

Torian narrowed his eyes.

She lifted her hands, balled her fingers into fists, and sat them on her slender hips. "You see, I don't remember asking your permission." She slanted a glance toward him. "I don't remember asking *anyone's* permission."

His mouth dropped open, and he was vaguely aware of the shocked gasps and exclamations that filled the room.

Sara's lip curved in apparent disgust. "You guys really have a lot to learn about women from my world." Her left eyebrow rose. "No one tells us what to do. We don't ask permission. We do…what we want." She swallowed. "And I want to save Bren."

Her cheeks were flushed and her eyes glittering. Her body was tense, her shoulders thrown back aggressively, her chin lifted high in the air. And she was beautiful. The most beautiful thing he'd ever seen in his life.

And she was about to die.

"No!" The room shook with the force of his fury. The lights flickered, dimmed. The floor rolled beneath them. "I won't allow—"

She turned on him. "You don't own me, Torian! You can't tell me what to do."

He pulled her into his arms and cradled her against his chest. She felt so slight, so delicate. *So precious.* "You're my mate," he whispered, wishing they were alone. "That means you belong to me." Why couldn't she understand that? She belonged to him. He belonged to her. For all time.

I have to do this. Her words slipped into his mind. *I can't stand back and let her die.* There was a flash of pain, hers, not his. And he saw her mother, broken and bloody, in a car. And he saw a young Sara helplessly trapped in the car. Watching her mother die.

I can't. He could feel the echoes of her grief. *I can't do it again. This time, I want to help. I want to save her.*

He closed his eyes against her plea. And he closed his mind. He couldn't stand her pain.

Her fingers touched his cheek. "Torian…" She spoke aloud this time, her voice whisper soft. "You've seen into me, as no other ever has." He opened his eyes and met her blue stare. Sara licked her lips and said, "I have to do this. Please try to understand."

The problem was, he did understand. He knew she didn't want to abandon Bren, didn't want to let the girl die.

And neither did he.

But he didn't want to risk Sara's life.

"I'm going. I'm going to this Rowena's Circle." Her jaw clenched. "I have to do this, Torian. I have to try and save her. And you—you can't stop me. I'm going to do this. I *am* going to save her."

And he knew he couldn't force her to stay at the manor, not without destroying the trust he was still so painstakingly trying to build. "Fine," he gritted, "but you aren't going alone."

"But they said—"

"Not alone," he snapped, thinking quickly. There was no way he was just going to hand his mate over to the Dark Ones. If Sara wanted to try and save Bren, then they would. But she would be protected at all times. Her life would be first priority.

He glanced at the others. "We don't have much time." And they would need to get all the power that they could. He was still weak from teleporting, and so were Blade and Fabian. They'd all have to pool their strength. "Gather your knives. Gather all the Trianium dust that you can find." The Trianium dust could be used against the Dark Ones. In mere seconds, it could burn away their flesh. And tonight he wasn't going to let any witches burn. But the Dark Ones, they were a whole different story.

"What are you planning?" Sara asked him, frowning.

"I'm planning on keeping you alive and killing them," he said bluntly, pressing a hard kiss to her soft lips. "Because there's no way in hell I'm losing you."

* * * *

The moon was almost full. Sara shivered as she stared up at the glowing light.

It was almost midnight. Time for the exchange. Time to trade her life for Bren's. Time to hope and pray that Torian's plan worked and that both she and Bren wound up free.

The sound of chanting drifted on the wind. She could hear the rise and fall of men's voices, hear the call of power. She was close to the area Torian had described as Rowena's Circle. He'd told her it had been named after a witch. A witch who'd been captured and burned on what should have been a sacred circle of land.

Sara sincerely hoped that same fate didn't await her.

She took a step forward, her feet crunching the leaves beneath her. So far, so good. Thanks to Torian and the other Guardians, the Dark Ones hadn't been able to sense her yet.

"The cloaking spell won't last long." Torian's voice drifted through her mind. *"The scent of the Becoming is too ripe on you. And your mark...they'll feel its pull soon. You'll have mere moments before the spell fades."*

And before every Dark One in the area sensed her.

Very carefully, she crept forward, her gaze drawn to the flickering flames in the middle of the clearing. The fire was orange, bright and strong. Around it, she saw a dozen men, all garbed in black robes. They were chanting, lifting their hands high into the air.

Damn. This did not look good. She reached into her own cloak and pulled out the knife Torian had given her. Like his, the hilt was encrusted with jewels. Rubies. Sapphires. Diamonds. He'd told her that the *Knias* was an enchanted weapon that could be used to kill a Dark One. She had a feeling she'd get to find out the truth of that statement very soon.

She glanced behind her. There was no sign of Torian or the other Guardians, but she knew they were there. In the darkness. In the woods. Watching. Waiting.

A girl's cry of pain and fear pierced the night. Sara jerked, a gasp of dismay rising in her throat. She'd been linked to Bren all night. Had felt the girl's mounting terror, her hopelessness. But something was different now. Something had changed.

What was happening? Sara scampered forward, trying to keep her body low to the ground, trying to stay in the shadows. Then she saw Bren being tied to a tall wooden pole in the middle of the circle. Men surrounded her, and then they started throwing branches at her feet.

Oh, shit. They were getting ready to burn her!

Sara knew she couldn't wait any longer. She had to act, now!

Taking a deep breath, she stood, stepped out of the shadows, and walked slowly into the clearing. At first, no one seemed to notice her. The men were too busy chanting. Too busy preparing to kill a helpless girl.

She stopped just inside the circle, cleared her throat, and

said, "I think you've been waiting for me." The men froze, and she looked down at her nails. "But, you know, if you're busy, I can always come back later."

Glancing up, she peered at them from beneath her lashes. Their white faces were lit with dark hunger. Their eyes were black, sunken.

The men surrounding Bren turned away from her and stalked toward Sara.

A smile curved her lips. She tilted her head back, looking fully around the camp now. "Well, looks like I've got everyone's attention." Not that it was a good thing to have all of them stalking her, but that had been the plan. She swallowed, choking down her fear. She wasn't going to let her mask slip. She wasn't going to let them see that she was so scared her knees were knocking together. "I'm here. Now let her go." Her thumb jerked toward Bren.

One of the men pushed back his hood. His features probably would have been considered handsome, if it weren't for the evil that seemed to ooze from his every pore. "Welcome, witch." His lips curled as his gaze drifted over body. "I didn't think the traitor would let you come."

The traitor? Her brow furrowed. Who was he talking about? "Look, buddy, let's just cut the small talk, okay? I'm here. I did my part. Now you do yours. Let the girl go." She could hear Bren crying, soft, pitiful cries that ripped at her heart.

The man threw back his head and laughed. His blond hair gleamed in the firelight.

She frowned at him. "Sorry, did I say something funny?" The guy was really starting to tick her off. And being scared and angry was not a good combination for her. She felt a humming tension sweep through her body.

The men circled her. She peered around, trying to see their faces, but she saw nothing but darkness. Evil.

"Why should we let her go?" Blondie asked. "This way, we get two for the price of one."

Sara inhaled sharply. "You know, Torian was right about you guys." Her fingers tightened around the knife.

"Oh? And what did our dear brother have to say about us?"

Brother? What the hell was the guy talking about? "He said that you'd pull some kind of stunt like this. That you'd go back on the bargain." Never trust a Dark One. That was going to be her new motto.

Blondie's lip curled. "And he let you come alone anyway? He always was a fool."

"Not exactly," she muttered, pulling the knife. Her fingers clenched around the shining hilt. Then she threw the knife, aiming straight for Blondie's chest. She heard a dull thud and a choked cry, but she didn't see him fall. She was already turning, raising the white powder to her lips and blowing.

Torian had taught her how to blow the powder, how to send the Trianium dust spiraling through the air. She did just as he'd instructed, sending it streaming toward the men.

Four of them vanished instantly, shrieking in agony. Then all hell seemed to break loose in the circle. The remaining Dark Ones swarmed her, their arms reaching out like snakes. She kicked out, catching one of the robed men in the kneecap.

Blue fire shot through the sky. The fire scorched another man, sending him crashing to the ground as he rolled, struggling to put out the hungry flames. Then the Guardians were there, fighting the Dark Ones. Knives flashed. Chants filled the air. White powder floated around them, drifting lazily through the air like smoke.

One robed figure lunged for her. Sara lifted her hand, feeling that strange humming tension spread through her. Damn. What was happening? She felt so—

A ball of white flames shot from her fingers, hitting the Dark One square in the chest. With a wrenching scream, he disappeared.

Her eyes widened. She looked at her palm. "Jesus." There was wonder in her voice. "What the hell did I just do?" And how the hell had she done it? Yesterday, she'd had to concentrate like crazy just to get a few sparks. Now, she was shooting flaming balls from her hand.

"Help!" Bren cried

Sara jerked around, her gaze searching through the smoke and bodies.

"Help!" Bren was struggling against her ropes, fighting to break free.

Sara ran toward her.

"Sara! Dammit, wait!" Torian called after her. She looked back at him, but he turned, fighting a Dark One who lunged at him with a knife.

A terror-filled scream rent the air. The branches near Bren's feet were on fire.

Oh, God. If she didn't do something, the girl would die. She glanced at Torian. He had the Trianium dust in his hand. The Dark One he'd been fighting lay beneath his feet, unmoving.

He was safe. But Bren—*she had to save Bren!*

She rushed forward, heedless of the smoking branches. "Hold on! I'm coming!"

The girl looked up at her, her face bruised and bloody. "Help me," she begged. "I d-don't want to d-die!"

"You're not going to die," she promised her, kicking at the branches. She reached behind Bren, struggling with the knots that bound her.

She could feel the fire, feel its hot breath on them. Bren was panting, moaning in fear, and the damn knots wouldn't budge.

"Break, damn you, break!" she screamed, and the ropes snapped in two. She blinked, and then a gurgle of surprised laughter slipped past her lips. "That's just—"

Bren screamed as the flames caught the hem of her dress. Sara grabbed her, jerking the girl away from the wood and the flames. Bren fell to the ground, and Sara crouched above her, slapping the smoldering fabric.

The wood was burning behind them, but Bren was safe. She was on the ground and tears were streaming down her face, but she was safe.

"We did it," Sara whispered, elation filling her. The Dark Ones were fleeing, vanishing into the night. Bren was safe. They'd won! They'd—

"Well, well. What do I have here?" There was a swirl of fog and then a man appeared. He had pale blond hair and silver eyes. Blue sparks danced in the air around him. "Two witches." He smiled, and a chill skated down her spine. "All alone."

"Sara!" Torian was running toward her, terror etched on his face. "Get away from him!"

She grabbed Bren, trying to pull her to her feet, but her body was a dead weight.

"Bren, get up!" she ordered, but the girl's eyes were closed and she wasn't moving.

"Sara!" Torian was closer now. The others were on his heels, thundering toward them. "Run!"

But she couldn't leave Bren. Couldn't save herself and leave the girl.

The man grabbed her arm and jerked her up beside him.

"Poor little witch…"

She kicked him as hard as she could, and he just laughed. His arms wrapped around her and he pulled her against his body. And she smelled death.

"I'm going to make you scream, little witch," he whispered, his breath burning her ear. "You'll beg me to kill you."

Her heart was pounding, the frantic drumming filling her ears. She tried to fight him, to break free, but his grip was too hard, too strong.

"Let her go, you bastard!" Torian yelled, skidding to a stop a few feet away.

The wizard holding her laughed.

Torian lifted his hand and a blue lightning bolt shot toward the dark wizard. But the Dark One lifted his hand and the bolt careened toward the sky.

His cloak lifted, wrapping around them.

"Torian!" she screamed, as desperate terror filled her.

"Say good-bye, witch," her captor muttered. "You'll never see your lover again."

"No! Sara!" Torian's voice was pierced with agony.

But she couldn't see him. All she saw was the blackness of the wizard's cloak. It was surrounding her. Suffocating her.

Killing her.

She struggled to breathe, to call Torian's name, but no sound emerged. The dark wizard pulled her tighter against him, whispered a spell, and then they vanished.

* * * *

"Torian, we have to leave." Fabian's voice was soft, his gaze filled with sadness.

Torian sat on the cold, hard earth, his stare pinned to the spot where he'd last seen Sara.

Sara.

She was gone. Taken from him.

"I should have saved her," he whispered, still seeing her face, still seeing the fear in her eyes. "I was supposed to take care of her." He swallowed. "But I let her go." He'd let that murdering bastard take her.

I'm sorry, Sara. I failed you.

The rising sun spilled golden light over the land, slowly forcing the dark shadows back. *Too late.*

"Now that they have her, the Dark Ones will gather tonight," Fabian said.

Yes, they would gather. They would drain Sara of all her precious magic. Her spirit. And then they would kill her. On the night he and she should have mated, on the night of the Becoming, they would burn her.

And rip his world apart.

"Why couldn't you have just stayed dead?" he muttered, still seeing his father's cruel smile. "Didn't hell want you?"

"We must prepare for the fight," Fabian continued, his voice subdued. "When we find them, we must be ready."

"I can't feel her," he whispered, staring at the blackened earth. "I can't touch her mind anymore. It's like she's—"

"No!" Fabian grabbed his arms and jerked him to his feet. "Don't say that. Don't even think it." His eyes were blazing. "Sara is not dead. Do you hear me? She's not!"

"But she will be," Blade said, coming to stand beside them. "Unless we find her by the rise of the moon."

Torian closed his eyes. "Why can't I touch her mind? Why can't I feel her?" He'd tried for hours to link with her, but he found only darkness. *Darkness.* Sara didn't like the dark.

His eyes snapped open, and he glared at his friends. "Don't you understand? If I can't touch her mind, I can't find her. The bastard could have taken her any damn where, but I can't find her. I don't know where she is."

"I do."

Torian spun around at the sound of that soft voice.

Bren stood before him, her head down and her body shaking.

"Bren? What did you say?"

She didn't look up. Her long black hair fell around her, hiding her face. "I know where the witch is."

He stepped toward her. "Look at me."

She shuddered and lifted her head. Her gray eyes were swimming with tears. "I-I heard them talking. I-I know what he w-wanted to do t-to her."

"What did you hear them say?" Torian gritted.

She licked her bruised and cracked lips. "S-she has the power they n-need. Th-they're going to take h-her power...like they d-did mine." The Dark Ones had drained nearly all of Bren's power. Just a whisper of her magic remained, the last remnant of her magical essence that they would have taken with her death.

"S-she's different," Bren whispered. "They s-said she was the one they'd b-been waiting f-for."

Yes, she was different. Special. But not just because of her magic. Because she was Sara. His Sara. Sweet. Beautiful. Good. *Sara.*

"Where were they taking her?" He kept his voice low, soothing. He could tell that Bren was barely holding herself together, and the last thing he wanted to do was shatter her delicate self control.

"The tower," she whispered. "The old tower in those ruins near the edge of the forest."

The ruins? He frowned. The castle had been built there centuries before, and all that was left of it now were old stones and the tower. A tall, steep tower, with crumbling steps and a window that seemed to look out over the very world itself.

"Why would they take her there?" Blade asked, shaking his head. "That's not a place known for dark magic."

The wizard who'd built the castle had been pure of heart. His magic had been good, light. He hadn't been tainted by the darkness.

Torian clenched his fingers into fists. "Maybe that's why. Because it's the last damn place we would think to look." Because when you searched for darkness, you never looked into the light.

"Are y-you going to f-find her?" Bren wasn't looking at him anymore. She was staring at the ground again, her hair a thin veil around her face.

"Yes," he swore, "I will."

"Good." Her hands trembled as she stroked the thin necklace that adorned her neck. "When you f-find h-her, tell her...tell her that I-I said thank you." A fat tear drop fell onto her hand. "She w-was with me, you know? Through the p-pain. I-I couldn't have m-made it, w-without her."

He stroked her shoulder. "I'll tell her," he said, his voice gruff. He ached for the pain the girl had endured, and he knew it would be a long time before she healed from the wounds she'd received.

He motioned toward Zane, and he stepped forward quickly to claim his sister. Torian waited until they'd walked out of sight before he turned to face his friends.

"When do we leave?" Blade asked.

"Now." He wouldn't wait another moment. They would storm the castle as soon as possible and reclaim his mate. He looked toward the sky. The sun was starting to rise, starting to light the sky.

The Dark Ones would be weak now. Many would be resting, hiding from the draining light. It was the perfect time to strike.

"Get the wizards," he ordered. "We're going after her." And he wouldn't stop until he had Sara back in his arms.

"What if it's not true?" Fabian asked softly. "What if the girl's lying?"

He shook his head. "She has no reason to lie." He knew that Fabian was suspicious of her. But then, Fabian was suspicious of everyone. He'd been that way, since Marie's death.

"It's not like the Dark Ones to make a mistake like this. Why would they tell her their plans?"

"They were going to kill her," he said bluntly. "They didn't care if she heard." But Sara had freed the girl from the flames. She'd saved her life, and now, it seemed, Bren might be doing the same for his sweet witch.

"Get the weapons," he ordered, knowing they would need all the power they could find, because Lazern was powerful enough to cheat death.

But Torian was determined that his father wouldn't get out of a second trip to hell. Yes, this time, he'd make damn sure the bastard was dead.

Hold on, Sara. He closed his eyes, and pictured her in his mind. Her sweet smile. Her shining eyes. *I'm coming for you.*

Twelve

Sara awoke to find herself lying on a hard stone floor, chained to the wall. Bright sunlight shot through a large window cut into the thick wall of ancient rock before her. The streaming sunlight hit her straight in the face.

Damn. As far as birthdays went, this was not turning out to be a good day.

She squinted and tried to look around. She was in some kind of large room. There was no furniture or rugs. The walls were made of large chunks of stone. And she was alone.

She jerked against the chains, trying to pull them from the wall, but there was no give to the restraints.

Great. Just great. She was chained up, held prisoner in God knew where, and as soon as the sun set, she was pretty sure she was going to die.

Happy birthday, indeed.

She rolled onto her side, wincing at the cramps and aches in her body. How long had she been here? The last thing she remembered was standing in the circle. The dark wizard had grabbed her and wrapped her in his cloak. She'd heard Torian's voice and then…

Nothing. The world had seemed to spin away from her, and she'd known only darkness.

Torian. Where was he? Was he all right? She prayed he was safe. Prayed that he'd managed to get the girl to safety.

And she prayed that she'd find some way out of the mess she was in.

Sara pulled against the chain, trying to slide her wrist out of the manacle. The metal cut into her flesh, digging deep. Blood rolled down her hand. She twisted, trying to yank her hand out, but it wouldn't move. The hold was too tight.

Dammit!

Her head fell back against the wall. She was so screwed.

Then she heard the thud of footsteps. Heavy, fast footsteps. Footsteps that were coming toward her. Getting close, and closer.

She tensed, remembering the link she'd shared with Bren. She'd felt the girl's pain as her powers were drained from her. Felt her agony, and she didn't want to feel it again. Didn't want to feel the Dark Ones rip her magic away from her. Didn't want—

The door banged open, crashing back against the stone wall. A man stood in the doorway, his body tall and strong. His face was hidden in shadow.

He stepped forward. "Sara?"

"Torian!" She would have known his voice anywhere. "Torian, thank God!" He'd found her. He'd come for her., and if she could just get out of those chains, she'd kiss him.

He rushed across the room, falling to his knees before her. "*Sara.*" His arms wrapped around her and he held her tightly. His body trembled against hers. "I thought I'd lost you," he muttered, his face buried in her hair.

She closed her eyes and inhaled his scent. Strong, masculine. Torian. He'd found her. Oh, God, the man was definitely her hero.

He pulled back, gazing down at her with his warm silver stare. "We've got to get you out of here." He eyed the chains, his gaze narrowing as he spied the blood still dripping down her hand. "Dammit, what did they do to you?"

"I did that." She grimaced. "I wanted to get out."

He tested the heavy metal of the chains, and his brows lowered. "These are wizard-forged. They're meant to hold witches."

Meant to hold witches. She didn't like the sound of that. Not. At. All. "Does that mean I can't get loose?"

His lips hitched into a tender half smile. "No, baby. It just means it takes a wizard's magic to break them." He lifted his hand and aimed a shower of blue sparks at the chain. The metal seemed to melt, freeing her instantly.

He lifted her hands, carefully inspecting the wound on her wrist.

"I'm all right," she whispered, wishing he'd pull her into his arms again. That'd he kiss her. "It's just a scratch."

He looked up, his gaze meeting hers.

She swallowed.

"I thought I'd lost you," he said, his voice thick. "I couldn't link with you. I couldn't find you."

"I-I think I was knocked out. I just woke up here a few minutes ago." And she really had no idea where "here" was.

He cupped her face in his warm, strong hands. "Don't ever scare me like that again," Torian ordered, his lips lowering toward hers. "When you disappeared with him..." He paused, his eyes darkening. "I didn't think I'd ever see you again."

"Torian…"

He kissed her. His lips were open, hot against hers. His tongue swept inside her mouth, teasing her, tasting her. Claiming her.

Raw hunger swept through her, hot and fierce. Her arms wrapped around him. She tried to pull him closer, desperate to feel his body against hers.

She didn't care that she was on a cold, hard stone floor. Didn't care that the sun was glaring down on her.

Torian was with her. His arms were wrapped around her, and his sensuous lips were on hers. Desire was beating through her. Heavy. Hard.

His lips lifted, and his eyes blazed down at her. There was hunger in his gaze, a hunger to match her own. And a stark need etched onto the hard lines of his face.

"Never again," he whispered, his voice a harsh growl. "I'm never letting you out of my sight again." His lips brushed against hers. "I'm going to keep you at my side, in my bed, and you're never getting away from me again."

That sounded pretty good to her. Right then, the idea of being in a big cushy bed with Torian sounded like heaven.

"Come on." He rose, pulling her to her feet. "Let's get out of here."

Her legs buckled when she tried to walk, and Torian grabbed her, lifting her high into his arms. He carried her down the stairs, holding her tightly.

"How did you find me?" She asked, tilting her head to look at him.

"Bren."

Relief swept through her. "Then she's all right."

He nodded. "She'd heard them talking and knew where they were going to take you." The steps narrowed, and he turned to his side, maneuvering carefully down the old stone.

"Remind me to thank her," she said, wondering what would have happened to her if Bren hadn't overheard the Dark Ones. What would they have done to her?

Stolen her powers. Burned her.

She closed her eyes, swallowing.

They were at the bottom of the stairs now. She could hear voices and footsteps.

"So you found our witch."

She opened her eyes and found Fabian staring down at her.

"Hello, Sara." He frowned at her. "Do me a favor. Don't ever disappear with Lazern again, okay? I don't think my heart can take it."

Neither could hers.

"What about the Dark Ones?" Torian asked. "Any sign of them?"

Fabian shook his head and said, "I think Sara was the only one here." He sighed. "I don't understand it. Why would they leave her unguarded? They had to know we'd be coming for her."

"But this is the last place they expected us to look." Torian's gaze swept across the ruins of the castle. "She was bound by wizard chains. There would have been no way for her to escape. They planned to keep her chained up until nightfall, and then..."

"Look, do we really need to paint him a picture?" Sara muttered when Fabian paled. "I think he gets the idea."

As she tried to rub her wrist, Fabian stared at her hand, his brows drawing together. "What happened?"

"I thought I could slide my wrist out of the manacle." She shrugged and tried not to wince at the burning ache in her wrist.

"I'll take care of you when we get home," Torian promised.

Home.

"You'll have to prepare," Fabian said, following them. "There's not much time left."

As Torian began walking carefully through the old stone ruins, Sara realized that she should protest. She should tell him her wrist was hurt, not her legs. She should say she was perfectly capable of walking and he didn't need to carry her.

And if it hadn't felt so damn good, so *right* to be in his arms, she would have told him to let her go. She wanted him to keep holding her, to keep making her feel safe. Protected. Loved. She hadn't felt that way before, not in a very, very long time.

"They'll try to stop you," Fabian's voice sounded from right behind her. She frowned, wishing he'd leave them alone for a moment. She'd had a hell of a night, and she really just wanted to rest.

Well, what she actually wanted was to curl up naked in a bed with Torian, and then she wanted to rest. What she did not want to do was think about the Dark Ones.

"They'll try," Torian agreed. "But they won't stop us."

Stop them from doing what? Vague curiosity stirred within her.

"We'll set up extra guards," Fabian said. "They won't get in to stop the ceremony."

The ceremony? What were they talking about now? Her eyes widened as comprehension swept through her. Today was her birthday. And the moon would be full tonight.

It was the time of the Becoming.

"Nothing will stop me." Torian's voice was hard. "And any Dark One who tries to get in my way will be destroyed."

The Becoming. *Tonight was the Becoming.*

What had he said? That she'd have to dance naked under the moon? "Uh, Torian?"

He kept walking, his arms tight around her. "We need to make certain the circle is prepared."

"Right." Fabian was beside them now. "Are you sure that you'll be able to handle…" He slanted a quick look toward her. "…everything?"

"Yes," Torian said with complete confidence.

"What about Lazern?"

His features hardened. "I'll deal with him."

There was such icy promise in his voice that Sara shivered.

"How did he come back?" Fabian whispered. "How did he survive?"

Good question. It had been quite a surprise to be kidnapped by a dead man.

"I don't know, but I'm damn well going to find out," he muttered. "Then I'm going to send him back to hell before he can hurt anyone else."

Like he hurt Bren, she thought. Like he'd hurt Fabian's sister. Like he'd almost hurt her.

If Torian hadn't found her…

She swallowed back the fear that rose in her throat. They were walking near a river. A dark, murky river.

"I'll get all the power that I need tonight," Torian said. "I'll be able to face him, to fight him. And this time, he won't get away."

"No, he won't," Fabian agreed, then slipped back, disappearing into the surrounding woods.

"He's the leader, isn't he?" She whispered. "He's the Dark One that's trying to take over, trying to destroy both your world and mine."

He nodded. "He has to be."

"But we're going to stop him, right?" She hoped they were

going to stop him. Because if they didn't, if Lazern was too powerful...then life as they knew it would end.

He looked down at her, his silver eyes bright with promise. "We sure as hell are."

She smiled, and his gaze dropped to her lips. His silver stare went molten. "But first we're going to mate. To Become." He took a deep breath. "I've waited so long for you. I've been going crazy with wanting you. Wanting to take you, to drive into your tight sex." He swallowed. "I can't wait to claim you."

Her heart raced. *Mate. Become.* She would bond with Torian. Make love with him. Finally.

"When the night falls," he whispered, his face tight with desire, "you're mine."

Thirteen

The moon, full, round and glowing, hung heavily in the night sky.

Sara stared up at the moon, marveling at its size. She'd never seen a moon so big, a moon that looked so close that she thought if tried, she just might be able to touch it.

"Sara…"

She turned from the window at the sound of her name. Fabian stood in her doorway, clothed in a white robe.

"It's time."

Her palms were damp. She took a deep breath and walked toward him. Her hand rubbed against her abdomen, against the birthmark hidden beneath her gown. The mark seemed to burn.

"Where's Torian?" She'd expected him to come to her room.

"He's waiting for you." His gaze swept down her body. "You look…lovely."

She felt her cheeks blush. "Uh, thanks." She was wearing a long, shimmering gown of white. Her feet were bare. She'd been told, by a very serious Torian, that the dress was the only thing she was supposed to wear. No shoes. No underwear. Nothing.

Fabian held open the door. As she walked past him, her gaze scanned the hallway. She could find no sign of the others who had been in the house just hours before. The home was silent, almost eerily so. The carpet cushioned their steps, and the only sound she heard was the faint whisper of her own breath.

"Don't be afraid," Fabian said, as he took her arm and led her down the stairs.

"I-I'm not." Terrified would be a better word. Hadn't Torian told her that there would be pain involved in this ceremony? Just how much pain had he been talking about?

"It's normal to be nervous before the Becoming," he continued, as if she hadn't spoken. "But it's been happening for centuries. It's our way."

But it wasn't hers. She cleared her throat, really not wanting to have this conversation with Torian's best friend. Things were awkward enough without this weird version of the birds and the bees. "Um…where is everyone?"

"Guarding the house. Wizards are stationed all around the perimeter." His face hardened. "No one will get inside. No one will stop the ceremony."

He led her to the back of the house, pushed open a heavy wooden door and stepped outside.

She hesitated.

"What is it?" His body tensed. "Do you sense something?"

She frowned at him. Since Blade had announced to the world that she was some kind of empath, the wizards had decided that she had some strange ability to "sense" everything that was happening in the world. They'd been asking her the same question all day long. She'd told them that she didn't sense a damn thing, but apparently no one believed her.

"Sara?"

"No, I don't sense anything," she muttered. "But I don't want to go out there if *he's* outside."

"He?" One brow lifted.

"Yeah, you know." Her gaze darted around the stone path. "Him. Daylon. The dragon."

Rich masculine laughter filled the night air. "Don't worry, sweet witch, the dragon's gone for the night."

She looked up, her breath catching. Torian stood at the end of the path. He was wearing all black, and he seemed to blend in with the very night itself.

Fabian slipped away, disappearing into the darkness.

She licked her lips and took a step forward. "I, uh, don't think I've ever heard you laugh before." And that was a real shame, too, because he had a wonderful laugh. Rich, masculine, strong.

"That's because I haven't had much to laugh about. My life has been too full of death and darkness for me to spend time laughing."

"Everyone should laugh." She took another step forward, her toes curling against the stone. "It's good for you."

"You're good for me," he whispered, lifting his hand, palm up, toward her. The shield on his wrist seemed to glow in the moonlight. "Come to me, Sara."

She swallowed. This was it. The big moment. There would be no going back. They would Become.

"I've been waiting for you." His voice carried easily through the night. "I've been waiting my whole life for you."

And she'd been waiting for him. She knew it deep inside. Knew that she'd been waiting to find him, to know him. To love him.

She walked toward him. He took her hand and brought it to his lips. His mouth pressed against the back of her hand. The stars shone down on them. The moon waited for them.

His gaze met hers. "Happy Birthday, Sara."

Her lips trembled into a smile.

"Do you come with me this night, willingly, to be my mate?"

"Y-yes." She knew there would be no going back now. Her future, her life, would be with Torian, her wizard.

His smile stole her breath. "Then come with me and let me show you a new world."

He led her down the stone path and into the waiting woods, the waiting night. He didn't speak as they walked. Just held her hand and moved carefully through the darkness. Crickets chirped in the distance, the faint bubble of a spring tickled her ears, and the perfume of the forest surrounded them, embraced them.

They approached a circle of stone. The moon shone directly overhead, reflecting off the shining stones. Torian turned to face her, cupping her chin in his warm hands. "Be very sure, Sara, because once you enter the circle, you won't be able to change your mind." His gaze searched hers, probing.

"I don't want to change my mind," she whispered. "I want to be with you."

"There are…things you don't know about me," he muttered. "Things I should have told you sooner, but I didn't want to scare you. I didn't want to lose you."

She put her finger against his lips. "I know everything about you that I need to know." He was strong. Brave. Honorable. *Hers.* She stroked the edge of his lips. "And I've made my choice. *You* are my choice."

He captured her wrist in his hand, pulling her palm down and pressing it against his chest. She could feel his heart racing, feel its frantic rhythm. "I don't deserve you," he whispered. "But I can't give you up. I need you too badly."

And she needed him.

She pulled her hand free of his grasp and moved back. After taking a deep breath, she lifted her fingers and untied the laces in the back of her gown.

This was it. The moment she'd been waiting for.

She shrugged her shoulders, and the gown slipped from her body with a soft rustle of sound. The warm night air blew over her bare flesh, and her nipples tightened in response.

She heard Torian inhale sharply. "I am supposed to be naked, right?" she murmured, moving toward the stones. "And I remember you telling me that I had to…dance."

His hand lifted, his fingers brushing against her nipple as she passed. Heat flashed through her at the touch, electrifying her.

"Yes…" The word sounded like a hiss.

She held her head high and walked into the circle. Standing naked before him, with the glow of the moon bathing her— well, it made her feel a little nervous, shy.

But it also made her feel a little naughty. A little wild.

She stood inside the stones, right in the center of the circle. Torian stood several feet away from her, his gaze locked on hers. Watching. Waiting. *Hungry.*

"A-are you sure that we're alone?" Being naked in front of Torian was one thing, but if any of the other Guardians were around…

He nodded, his gaze never leaving hers. "They're protecting the grounds. No one's here but us."

"Good." She realized that her hands were shaking.

"Dance for me," he whispered, his voice floating on the night.

Her eyes widened. "I-I don't know how."

"Move for me. Move your body, your hips. Offer yourself to me." His voice was rougher now, laced with the fine edge of hunger.

He walked toward her. No, he stalked toward her, his gaze intent, and he jerked off his shirt, tossing it onto the ground. "Do it, Sara. Dance for me."

The crickets had stopped calling, and she couldn't hear the spring anymore. She couldn't hear anything but Torian's rough velvet voice and the sound of her own pounding heart.

He was close to her now, so very close. She could smell his masculine scent. Could feel the heat of his stare upon her skin. He lifted his hand and his fingers rubbed against her breast. She gasped at the contact.

He trailed his fingers down her stomach, and then he slid both hands around to rest against the curves of her hips. "Do it," he repeated, his voice nearly a growl. "Dance for me." His fingers tightened against her bare skin, pressing against her, urging her to move.

So she did. A soft, undulating roll of her hips.

His nostrils flared. "Again. More."

And that wildness flared again within her. She stepped forward, sliding her leg between his. Her hips rolled, shifting lightly from side to side, as her body moved against his, on his.

It felt good. Deliciously good. She wanted to do it again.

Sara lifted her arms, holding them high over her head, and she rubbed against him, stretching sensuously. Her nipples slid across his chest, slid across his hot flesh.

Then she slipped around him, closing her eyes.

And she danced, her hips undulating and her arms lifting, reaching for the stars, for the moon. Her hips moved in a slow circle. Her hands slid down her body, cupping her breasts. Offering them to him. Offering her body to him.

And she danced. An ancient rhythm. A sexual call. A mating ritual.

Her feet moved against the soft earth. Her hands moved gracefully, fluidly. Her hand trailed down his cheek, her palm stroked his skin. She turned away from him, swaying her hips as she moved. She glanced over her shoulder at him, shifting her body in a gentle rhythm.

She'd never danced for anyone before. Never stood naked in the moonlight. She'd never known how good it would feel. How free. She'd never known how sensual her own body would seem.

She tilted her head back, thrusting her breasts forward. Her body was aching, yearning. And the movement of the dance only increased her need for him.

Torian.

Her gaze flashed to meet his. His jaw was clenched, and his stare—so hot, so hungry—was on her.

Her hips rolled once more, a slow dip, and her gaze slid down his body. Down the muscled expanse of his bare chest. Down to the top of his black pants. Down...

She could see his desire. See the hard strength of his arousal pushing against the front of the fabric. And she knew that he liked her dance. Knew that she aroused him, and it made her feel powerful. Desirable. Seductive.

She wasn't the woman that Tom had called cold. She was a woman who was hungry. A woman who was burning with desire.

She glided closer to Torian, never taking her eyes from his. She rubbed her body against his, pressing her hips against the bulge of his arousal. He felt hard, thick against her.

And she couldn't wait to feel him *in* her.

She slid her hands down his body, pressed against his shaft and stroked.

He groaned, his eyes closing, and she smiled. "Did you like my dance?" Her fingers caressed him.

His erection flexed beneath her touch, lengthening even more.

Sara lowered her body before him, moving lightly, slowly. Her knees touched the soft earth and she unhooked his pants.

"Did you?" she asked, slowly lowering his zipper. She wanted to see his bare flesh under the glowing light of the moon. She wanted to touch him. To taste him.

She freed his heavy arousal, trailing her fingertips over its broad tip. He inhaled sharply, and she looked up at him through her lashes. "I think you did," she whispered. "I think you liked it very much..." Leaning forward, she took him into her mouth.

He shuddered against her, and his fingers wrapped around her shoulders, clenching against her skin.

Her tongue swept over him, tasting him, stroking him.

"Sara..." Her name was gritted between clenched teeth. "Sara...that feels...so damn...good."

She licked his broad tip, her fingers wrapping around his shaft. Her tongue swept across the head of his arousal, and she felt him jerk against her.

"Witch," he muttered. "You're driving me out of my mind..."

His hands slid under her arms and he lifted her from her knees, settling her body against his. His mouth swept down to claim hers. His tongue pushed into her mouth. Teased her. Stroked her. And made her want more.

He tore his mouth away from hers and kissed a fiery trail down her neck. She gasped, heat coiling in her belly. His arms were wrapped around her, his right hand squeezing her buttocks. His arousal nudged her thighs, rubbing against her hungry flesh.

Her knees buckled and she grabbed his arms, trying to hold on to him. He laughed, and lowered her to the ground, pausing only long enough to completely strip his body.

Torian rose above her, the moon and a million stars shining behind him. "It's time," he whispered, before lowering his head to lick the curve of her breast.

A moan rumbled in her throat when his tongue swirled over her areola. Her back arched. Then he started to suck her, to lick—oh, God, the man sure had a way with his mouth.

His legs pushed between hers, parting her thighs, opening her to his touch, and his broad fingers parted her folds.

"Are you ready for me?" he murmured, turning to give her

other breast the same tender attention.

He pushed one finger into her, testing her.

She lifted her hips, pushing against him. "Torian!" Oh yeah, she was ready. More than ready. She needed *him*.

"Ah...you're so wet for me...and hot." There was rich satisfaction in your voice.

Her body was flooded with sensation. Need. Desire. A heavy tension coiled within her. She wanted him, wanted him to thrust into her body, hard and deep. She wanted to feel his thick length inside of her. *Now.*

His thumb stroked her, pressing against the center of her need. She gasped, her eyes widening as pleasure shot through her from just that simple touch.

He smiled. "We're going to be so good together." His tongue licked her nipple. "So good."

She was panting, Sara realized. Lifting her hips, straining against him. And she didn't care. Her body was on fire. And only he could satisfy her. Only Torian.

She felt the head of his shaft pressing against her, felt him ease just a bit inside her tight passage.

"Sara, look at me."

Her gaze jerked up. His eyes were feverishly bright. His jaw was locked, and his face was full of naked hunger.

"Torian..." *She wanted him inside of her.*

"From this moment on, we're joined. One heart. One soul. One power." A trickle of sweat ran down his brow. She felt the stiffness of his muscles. His hands lifted, his fingers locking with hers.

And his arousal pressed against her.

"Are you ready?" He whispered. "Are you ready for me?"

Her body was tight with need, yearning. She didn't think she could wait any longer. She had to have him, inside, thrusting, filling her. "Yes..."

She could see the moon above him, see the sparkling glitter of the stars. And she could see his eyes, eyes that seemed to gaze straight into her very soul.

"Then take me..." He thrust deep, burying his shaft completely in her.

The world exploded into a blinding shower of light. Pleasure rocked through her. She moaned, feeling every muscle in her body tighten in immediate response. She could hear a faint humming, could feel energy pulsing around her, through her.

And she could feel him. Torian. Feel him inside her body...

and inside her mind.

The light vanished, and dozens of images flashed in front of her eyes. She saw a young boy, running with tears streaming down his cheeks. She saw him falling before the smoldering embers of a fire. Saw him throw back his head and scream in anger, in pain.

She saw the same boy, older, standing in a circle of men, all wearing black robes. She saw Lazern hitting the boy, hitting the boy...hitting *Torian*.

Oh God, that boy—he was Torian!

Then she saw the man that Torian was. Saw him fighting Lazern. Saw him pulling out his knife. Saw him stab the dark wizard. Saw the blood pool between them.

She saw everything. His life. His mind. His thoughts were hers. His dreams—hers. His nightmares—hers.

For one incredible moment, she became him.

Torian.

Light flashed, and the images burned away. A fiery blast of power shot through her, jerking her body.

"Torian!" She felt like she was in a storm-tossed sea. There was no anchor for her. Magic, power, thundered through her body, her mind, and she was terrified. It was too much. The feelings. The magic. Too much. She couldn't stand it, couldn't take it anymore. She screamed.

I'm here, his voice whispered through her thoughts. *I'm with you. I'll never leave you.*

A quiet calm crept through her. The burning power slowly faded and the bright light disappeared. She could see the night once again. Could see the stars, the moon.

Could see Torian.

Torian. He was still buried in her body. His heavy arousal filled her, stretched her.

Her hands were shaking against his. "I-is it...over?" She asked, a tremor in her voice.

He shook his head. "The pain is," he whispered, leaning down to press a hot, open-mouthed kiss to her lips. "But the pleasure is just starting."

And he began to thrust. His body moved, hard and strong, against her. His left hand released hers and moved down her body, stroking her sensitive core.

She forgot the pain. Forgot the burning power that had scorched her. And she felt the passion, felt the desire, sweep through her once again.

Her body tightened, her delicate inner muscles clenched around him. She lifted her hips, wrapped her legs around him, and matched him thrust for thrust. Pleasure pulsed through her, building higher and higher. Her head thrashed against the soft earth. Her body strained. She wanted to get closer to him. Closer...

His mouth locked on her breast. Licked. Sucked. And it felt so good. So unbelievably good.

He lifted his head and licked his lips. His silver gaze was blazing. His hips thrust against her. Deep. Demanding.

"Come for me," he gritted. "Let me see your pleasure."

His hands locked on her hips. He lifted her, forcing her to take even more of him.

She moaned, her body clenching.

"Come..."

Her climax ripped through her, and she choked out his name, her body shuddering with the fierce force of her orgasm.

Dimly, she was aware of him tensing against her. Aware of the harsh groan that slipped past his lips.

His arms wrapped around her, pulling her close to him, close to his heart.

Her breathing was ragged. Her body drifting in bliss. And, damn, she felt wonderful. She kissed his shoulder.

Torian. Her wizard.

"I love you," she whispered, the words tumbling from her in a quick rush.

His head jerked up. His cheeks were still flushed, and his eyes widened as he stared down at her in disbelief. "What?"

She licked her lips, realizing what she'd just admitted. Oh, damn. The afterglow had gotten to her. Lowered her guard. She hadn't meant to tell him that. Not yet.

But it was too late for regrets. Too late to pretend she hadn't just told him the words she'd been keeping secret. He was staring at her now like he thought she was crazy. Great. Just great.

"Sara? What did you say?" His voice was incredibly soft.

She swallowed. Oh, well, it was now or never. "I said that I love—"

A ball of fire shot through the air, landing in a smoldering heap right next to them, and the sound of laughter, loud and maniacal, filled the air.

And Lazern stepped into the circle of stones.

Fourteen

Torian moved in a blur, jumping to his feet and standing protectively over Sara. He waved his hand toward her, dressing both of them with an instant spell.

Lazern smiled at him. "Hello, son."

"Don't call me that," he spat, his hands clenching.

Lazern's eyes narrowed. Then he looked over Torian's shoulder, his gaze landing on Sara.

Torian stiffened and took a step forward.

"I see you've gotten yourself bonded to a High Witch." Lazern's lips curved downward, as if in distaste. "Pity. I'd hoped to arrive before the...festivities got underway." He pointed at Sara. "You're as strong as I thought you'd be. Your powers are in the air. I can feel them calling to me."

"Yeah," Sara muttered, glaring at him. "And if you don't get out of here that's not all you'll be feeling."

Lazern laughed, a harsh, grating sound. "Oh, my dear, you don't scare me. Nothing scares me." His smile vanished. "But I do like your spirit. It's always so much fun to break a witch's spirit." He slanted a look toward his son. "Isn't it, Torian? You remember what it was like, don't you?"

Torian felt shame burn through him.

"Did he tell you?" Lazern asked Sara. "Did he tell you about all of the wonderfully wicked things he did when he was a Dark One?"

"Shut up," Torian snarled, sending a bolt of pure magic toward Lazern's chest. "Just shut the hell up!" He didn't look at Sara. Couldn't look at her.

Lazern staggered back beneath the blow, and his silver stare flashed black. "That wasn't nice, *son*." A ball of blue fire appeared in his hands. "Not nice at all. Show some respect for your elders." He threw the ball, aiming straight for Torian's head.

Torian grabbed Sara and jumped to the side. He felt the brush of fire against his skin. "Blade, Fabian!" he called out to the other Guardians, knowing they would be nearby, waiting.

Lazern tilted his head to the side, as if listening to something. Or someone.

An icy chill slid through Torian. He knew that look. Knew that satisfied twist of Lazern's lips. *Blade, Fabian, answer me!*

But there was no answer to his mental call.

"What did you do?" He growled, feeling rage burn hotly in his belly.

Lazern shrugged. "Why don't you go find out?" His gaze raked down Sara's body. "And I'll just stay here and keep your...witch...happy." Fire began to flicker near his hand. "Tell me, witch, do you like flames?"

Sara's hand locked on Torian's, her nails digging deep. "There are others here," she whispered. "I can feel them. The Dark Ones. They're all around."

Damn. That was why Blade and Fabian weren't answering his call.

"How did you get past the Guardians?" he asked Lazern.

The fire flared brighter, the flames reflecting in Lazern's eyes. "Magic."

"You know, Torian," Sara muttered, "no offense, but your old man's a bastard."

Lazern laughed. "Killing you will be so much fun..."

She barred her teeth at him. "Think so? Then why don't you come and give it a try?"

What was she doing? Torian jerked her behind him, trying to shield her. *Don't draw his attention,* he ordered.

Why the hell not? she snapped right back. *We're stronger than him, I can feel it. We can take him.*

"No," Lazern said very deliberately, "you can't." And he shot the glowing ball of flames into Torian's chest.

Burning pain pierced him. He fell to the ground, twisting and shaking as agony lanced through him.

Sara screamed. He felt her soft hands upon his cheek, but he couldn't move, couldn't call out to her. He could only lay there and feel the whisper of death upon his skin.

"Fool," Lazern muttered, coming to glare down at him. "You were never stronger than me. You'll never be stronger than me, even with your witch's help." He grabbed Sara's arm and yanked her to her feet.

She kicked Lazern's shin. He didn't even flinch.

Torian stared up at them, fear lashing him as he saw Sara in Lazern's arms.

Sara!

* * * *

She could feel Torian's pain, feel his anguish lapping at her. Oh, God, she had to help him! Sara twisted, squirming in Lazern's hold, trying to break free, to—

Lazern's hand wrapped around her throat. Blue sparks slid

around her body.

"Do you know how many witches I've killed?" Lazern's fingers tightened around her neck.

The pain of Lazern's touch burned her. Her throat was closing, the air being slowly choked from her, and she was afraid that death was coming for her. Afraid that it was coming in the darkness...coming to claim her.

Lazern laughed, his stare trained on her like a hungry hawk. She stared back at him, back into those soulless eyes. She wouldn't let him see that she was afraid. Wouldn't let him know that she was utterly terrified. He'd hurt Torian. Hurt him badly. She could see him from the corner of her eye. He wasn't moving. He was lying on the ground, his silver eyes locked on her, and he wasn't moving.

Oh, God. He'd been wrong. She'd been wrong. Lazern was too powerful. Even with the Becoming, they wouldn't be able to stop him.

He leaned down, whispering in her ear. "How many did I kill?" he asked again. Then, with a kind of wicked glee, he said, "I can't even remember myself anymore." His breath was hot against her. "After the first thirty, I stopped counting."

Sara closed her eyes. No wonder he was so strong. He'd drained so much power from his victims. He'd *stolen* so much power.

"But you know what I do remember?" His fingers were crushing her larynx. She couldn't breathe, couldn't fight. "Their screams. They had such wonderful screams."

She forced herself to open her eyes and look at the monster that held her. He was smiling, his thin lips curved. His eyes were so very cold, and she knew she was looking at the face of death.

Poor Torian. To have grown up with this—this *thing* as his father.

"Are you ready to burn?" He asked.

Her throat was already burning, and a numbness was spreading in her hands, her feet. He tossed her to the ground.

"But first, let's have a taste of that power, shall we?" He licked his lips. "It's been so long since I've had a High Witch." His contemptuous gaze flickered to Torian's prone body. "Not since I drained his mother's power."

And Torian had been there, she realized. The images she'd seen suddenly made terrifying sense. The boy who'd cried, who'd fought. The boy who'd wept over the smoking embers.

Her heart ached as she realized his mother had burned, at his father's hands. *Oh, Torian, I'm so sorry.* So sorry for the pain he'd endured. The heartache.

And she knew she couldn't let him suffer anymore, couldn't let Lazern hurt him again.

She pushed herself up, managing to stagger to her feet. "You want a taste?" She tossed back her head. "Then come and get it." Her voice was weak, husky.

He lifted his hand, and she felt the rush of his power. Lazern's lips were curving, and she knew he was going to strip the power from her, to steal her magic. She pulled back her hands, reaching for the strength of the magic that had been unlocked within her, and it was there, waiting for her. Shining, strong and bright.

"Here's your taste," she muttered, and launched the ball of magic at him.

His eyes widened and he stepped back. The golden light slammed into him, driving straight into his chest. He moaned, falling to his knees.

She ran past him, crouching beside Torian. Her hands flew over him. His shirt was burned, his chest stained with soot. But there was no wound that she could see. At least, not on the outside.

"Torian?"

His eyes blinked. He opened his mouth, tried to speak, and a low groan emerged from his throat.

"It's all right," she whispered. "Everything's going to be all right."

His eyes widened. He groaned again, his lips twitching.

"Relax, okay? I'll go get help—*Ah!*" Her words ended in a scream as she was grabbed by her hair and pulled to her feet.

"You'll pay for that, witch." Lazern's face was stark white. His eyes were blacker than the night. "I'll make you beg for the fire to consume you."

He pushed his hand against her heart, and she whimpered as a lancing pain pierced her body. And then an icy cold spread through her chest. Light began to flash around his hand as he chanted, and she knew that he was draining her, that he was taking her magic.

She tried to push against him, tried to summon her power, but her arms were limp and she couldn't feel her magic. Couldn't feel it anymore. She could only feel his cold touch, like ice against her heart, her soul.

"I'm going to drain you dry, witch," he muttered, and the light around his hand shot into her body.

She screamed, her stomach convulsing. The pain was blinding, like a knife cutting into her over and over. Oh God, he was ripping her apart!

She knew this pain, remembered it. *Bren.* He'd drained Bren, then left the girl to die. Just as he was going to do with her.

Her heart was stuttering. She could feel it, feel it struggling to beat.

They had failed. Lazern was going to win. Black dots danced before her eyes.

She'd tried to tell Torian that she wasn't the one. Wasn't the one who'd save their worlds. Hell, she couldn't even save herself.

"Don't worry, my dear. After I burn you," he said, his breath brushing against her cheek, "I'll send my son to join you in the flames."

She stiffened. *No.* No, she couldn't let that happen. He couldn't hurt Torian. She *wouldn't* let him.

"He was always such a disappointment to me." Lazern shook his head. "You know he actually tried to stop me from killing those witches? He fought me, his own father!"

"That's...because..." She sucked in a sharp breath and tried to gather the remains of her strength. "He's...good."

"Good." His lip twisted in distaste. "Weak, that's what he is. What he's always been."

"No." Her body felt like it was encased in ice. "He's...strong."

"Oh?" His hand pressed harder against her heart and she flinched. "Then why isn't he saving you?"

"I am," Torian growled.

Her gaze shot past Lazern and locked on Torian. His face was pale with strain, but power seemed to glow from his silver eyes.

Torian grabbed Lazern, jerking him away from her.

Sara fell to the ground, choking, coughing, and shuddering with pain.

Torian stood over his father, his body trembling. "You shouldn't have touched her." He took a step forward. "You should *never* have touched her." He lashed out, sending a ball of blue flames flying through the air.

Lazern lifted his head, and with a toss of his hand, the flames disappeared. "Is that the best you've got?"

"No," Torian snarled, his eyes narrowing. "This is." And he sent a bolt of blue lightning at Lazern.

Lazern's scream echoed through the night as the light blasted into him, burning deep into his flesh. He fell to the ground, his body convulsing.

"This time," Torian promised, "I'm going to make sure that you're dead."

Lines of pain were etched onto Lazern's face. "You'd kill me...your own father...for a witch?"

"My father's dead!" he snarled. "He died the day he touched darkness, the day he killed my mother."

Sara dragged her body up and stumbled toward him. "Torian..." Her arms wrapped around his body, and she held onto him, desperate to feel him, to make certain he was safe. God, she'd nearly lost him!

"I raised you," Lazern snapped, gritting his teeth as he tried to rise.

"You tortured me. You beat me. Starved me. And when I wouldn't join you in the darkness, you tried to kill me." There was hate in Torian's voice. Hate. Fury. Pain.

Lazern was on his knees now. "You threw away the power that I could have given you."

"I didn't want anything of yours." His hand tightened around Sara's.

Lazern stood, slowly stretching his body. His clothes were burned, his skin charred. "You can't kill me. I'm your blood."

"I did it before." He drew a deep breath. "I'll do it again."

Lazern's shirt was all but gone. Beneath the soot, Sara could see the long, white scar that ran the length of chest.

"I'm too strong." Lazern lifted his hands. "Nothing can stop me!" He laughed. "Your witch is too weak to help you, and soon, when you're dead on the ground, I'll finish with her. I'll suck every ounce of power from her body."

Sara, link with me. Open your mind and share your magic. Torian's voice was soft in her mind, a bare whisper.

I'm so tired, Torian. So tired... Her muscles were shaking.
Stay strong. Do it for me. Help me.

She swallowed. Her fingers twined with his. Blue flames danced around them. She reached deep inside, past the pain, past the ice. *For you.*

Golden light circled the flames. Burned with them. Flared brighter.

"No!" There was fear in Lazern's voice, on his face. "You can't—"

His voice ended in a choked cry of rage as they launched their magic at him. The light wrapped around him, sunk into him.

Sara heard voices then. Dozens of voices. Women's voices. Soft and soothing. Loud and shrill. Chanting. All chanting. And she saw faint red lights rise from Lazern's body, saw him twist, spasm. Again and again, the spasms shook his body.

The red lights floated into the sky, drifting higher and higher. One of the red lights flew toward them, circling Torian. Then in a flash, the lights vanished.

Lazern lay on the ground, face down. His arms were spread in front of him. His body was still, stiff.

Torian pulled her into his arms. "Sara…" His hold tightened. "I thought I was going to lose you."

"No." She kissed him. "That's never going to happen." He felt so good against her. Strong. Steady. *Alive.*

"We did it," she whispered. "We actually did it." And she could hardly believe it.

His lips curved. "Was there ever any doubt?"

She lifted one brow. "Well…"

"Torian, Sara, look out!" Blade's cry cut through the night.

They turned and saw Lazern, standing with a knife in his fist. He smiled and blood pooled down his lips. "You took my magic…now I'm going to take your life." He lunged for them.

Sara lifted her arm, preparing to strike at him. A ball of blue fire appeared in Torian's hands, and Fabian leapt forward from the darkness, a jeweled knife in his hand.

"Lazern!" Fabian screamed. "Lazern!"

The Dark One turned toward him.

"This is for my sister, you bastard!" Fabian threw his knife, and it rolled end over end in a sickening blur toward Lazern. There was a dull thud as it landed, embedding itself deep in Lazern's chest.

The Dark One sank to his knees, his own knife falling from his fingers. His lips curved. "You…can't kill…me."

Torian stepped forward. "Yeah, we can." Blue fire erupted from his fingertips.

Lazern vanished, disappearing into a ball of flame.

* * * *

It was over, Torian realized. It was finally over. The Dark Ones had been defeated. Even now, the Guardians were chasing down the last of the evil wizards.

Lazern had been their leader. Without him, they were lost, their magic weak. They would be no match for the Guardians on their trail.

Yes, it was finally over.

He paced along the hallway in his home, his gaze moving to the closed bedroom door. Sara was in there. She'd gone upstairs while he briefed the others. She'd told him that she needed some time to herself, some time to think.

Hell, she'd almost been killed tonight. She'd seen him kill his own father. She probably had a damn lot to think about.

His hands balled into fists. He'd put her in danger. Nearly gotten her killed. If her own powers hadn't been so strong, they never would have survived the battle.

Lazern would have destroyed her. Drained her, burned her—

The door jerked open. Sara stood on the other side, glowering at him. "Could you stop obsessing over that?" She snapped. "I can't get a decent moment's rest because your thoughts keep slamming into my head."

He flushed. "Ah...sorry."

She crossed her arms over her chest. "And for the record, you're not to blame for anything that happened tonight. In fact, if it hadn't been for you, I would be dead."

He stepped toward her. "He was my father. You don't know the things that—"

She closed the space between them, her face softening. "Yes, I do know. I know everything." Her lips curved. "We're bonded, remember?"

Oh, yes, he remembered the bonding. Remembered the feel of Becoming with her. Remembered the flood of memories that had swept through him. Seeing her mother pinned in the car. Her mother's funeral.

He'd seen her standing all alone by a river, tears coursing down her cheeks. He'd felt her. Her thoughts, her emotions. He'd seen into her. Become her. As she'd Become him.

"So you know...what I did."

Her brows furrowed, and shame burned through him. He hated that she knew that he'd become a Dark One.

He'd touched the dark power, felt it creep into his soul. It was his secret disgrace, his horror, and he knew it made him unworthy of her. Of her love.

She'd thought that he was good, but there was a darkness in him. A darkness that went down to his very soul. And he couldn't let that darkness touch her. Couldn't let it touch her light.

He would have to send her away. "Sara...you know what I'm like. You know my darkness."

Her lips compressed. "I felt it that first time...back at the cabin." She swallowed. "I saw it then, when I linked with you."

"It's been with me for as long as I can remember. Ever since..."

"Your mother died," she finished softly. "*I know, Torian.* I saw what he did to her...to you."

"I wanted to save her," he whispered, seeing the past. "I tried to get to her, but the fire was too hot." He lifted his hands, remembering the blisters and burns that had covered his skin for months after that terrible night. "And then it was too late. She was gone."

And he'd been left alone with Lazern. For all of those years, he'd been with him. "He tried to make me like him," he whispered. "Tried to get me to use the dark magic." And though he'd fought, the darkness had crept into him, slid past his guard.

He took her hands in his, pulling her to him. "I swear to you, I never killed a witch. I hated what he did. I tried to stop him, to save those women..."

"I know," she said, her voice soft. "I know what you did." Her eyes were shimmering. "You were just a child, Torian. He tried to change you, to make you evil. But he couldn't because you're good. Strong."

He shook his head.

"Yes, you are." Her shoulders lifted as she took a deep breath. "I've felt the darkness in you. I know it's there. But so is the light. The goodness. Torian, there is so much goodness in you. So much strength. I can see it, every time that I look into your eyes."

"But what if I change?" He asked, voicing the fear that had plagued him his whole life. "What if I become like him?" That was his nightmare, the fear that haunted him every night. And if he turned and he hurt Sara...

"You won't," she said with absolute certainty. "You can't." Her fingers twined with his. "The darkness in you is chained. You control it, not the other way around. And I know, *I know,* that you'll never be like him. You couldn't be."

"I don't want to hurt you," he said, his voice roughening. "If I ever did anything to you..."

"Oh, Torian, that's not going to happen." Her gaze was

solemn. "I've seen into you. Into your heart, your soul. And believe me, there's nothing evil there." She smiled at him. "The man I love isn't evil."

He stilled. She'd said it again. *Love.* Hope began to grow within him. Could she really love him? "Sara, I took you from your home, your world—"

"And you gave me a new one," she said, her stare bright, steady. "I was alone. Then you came along, and for the first time in years, I truly felt alive." She paused and then said, "I love you, Torian le Fury."

He'd hoped, prayed, that one day she would say those words to him. That she'd come to care for him, to love him, had been his wish from the beginning. "Sara..."

The brightness dimmed from her eyes. "I'm not asking you to love me back. I just wanted you to—"

He kissed her, kissed her with all the hunger and love that he possessed. And she felt so good, so right, against him. Like a dream come true. Like magic.

He lifted his head. "How could I not love you?" He kissed her again, because he had to taste her sweet lips. "Woman, I've loved you since the first moment I saw you." He stroked her silken cheek. "You were so brave then, swinging that flashlight at me." His lip curled. "Telling me to get the hell out of your house."

"Oh, yeah," she teased, her voice light. "I can see where that would have put you in a loving mood."

"It did. You did." He gazed into her eyes, needing her to understand, needing her to realize how important she was to him. "You're so brave, Sara. You take life with both hands, and you hold on, no matter what comes your way." She was the strongest woman he'd ever known. The most courageous. "It was easy to love you," he whispered, the words honest, stark. "So damn easy. I love you, Saralynn Myers. You're my mate, my heart.

She swallowed. "And you're the man I love." A lone tear slid down her cheek. "My wizard." She pulled his head down toward her and pressed her lips against his.

He could taste the sweetness of her love in the kiss. And when he lifted his head, he saw his future shining in the depths of her brilliant blue eyes. He'd found his witch, his mate, and he would never let her go.

Epilogue

"You know, I don't remember anyone telling me it would hurt this much," Sara gritted, her teeth clenched. She glared at Torian, completely blaming him for the agony that was currently ripping her apart.

He flushed. "I'm sorry, if I had known—"

She groaned, a long, guttural cry that was ripped from her.

His hands clenched into fists. "Can't you do anything for her?" he asked the doctor, and Sara wondered if the bespectacled man saw the blue sparks that were dancing in the air.

The doctor frowned at him. "The baby is—"

"Coming!" She gasped out as another contraction seized her. "It's coming now!" She grabbed Torian's hand, squeezing for all that she was worth.

And in seconds, her baby was there. Her loud cry announced her arrival to the world. There were tears in Torian's eyes and a smile on his face.

Sara decided that she would forgive him for the pain that she'd just gone through as she took her baby in her arms.

A little angel stared back at her. An angel with blue eyes and black hair. Blue sparks danced around the room.

"Torian," she whispered. "Stop it! The doctors are going to notice."

His thumb was stroking the baby's cheek. "Notice what?"

She jabbed him in the ribs, jerking her head toward the sparks.

His eyes widened and his smile stretched even farther. "That's not me."

What? If it wasn't him…

Sara glanced down at the baby—at her innocent blue eyes, and at her soft bow lips.

The sparks danced into the air.

She pushed back the blanket and stared at her daughter. There was a birthmark on her abdomen. A birthmark in the shape of a sword.

The baby cooed softly, and as the sparks disappeared, the sound of Torian's delighted laughter filled the room.